CANDIDE

CANDIDE

VOLTAIRE (PEN NAME)

FRANÇOIS-MARIE AROUET

KALPAZ

ISBN: 978-93-5128-565-6

First Published in 1759
Indian Reprint in 2017

Published by

Kalpaz Publications
C-30, Satyawati Nagar,
Delhi – 110052
E-mail: kalpaz@hotmail.com
Website: kalpazpublications.com
Ph.: +91-9212142040

Cataloging in Publication Data—DK
Courtesy: D.K. Agencies (P) Ltd. <docinfo@dkagencies.com>

Voltaire, 1694-1778, **author.**
[Candide. English]
Candide / Voltaire (pen name) Franc'˜ois-Marie Arouet.
pages cm
Novella.
Translated from French.
Translation of: Candide.
"First published in 1759"—Title page verso.
ISBN 9789351285656

1. French fiction—Translations into English. I. Title.

PQ2082.C3E5 2017 DDC 843.5 23

TABLE OF CONTENTS

CHAPTER 1

How Candide Was Brought Up in a Magnificent Castle and How He Was Driven Thence

In the country of Westphalia, in the castle of the most noble Baron of Thunder–ten–tronckh, lived a youth whom Nature had endowed with a most sweet disposition. His face was the true index of his mind. He had a solid judgment joined to the most unaffected simplicity; and hence, I presume, he had his name of Candide. The old servants of the house suspected him to have been the son of the Baron's sister, by a very good sort of a gentleman of the neighborhood, whom that young lady refused to marry, because he could produce no more than threescore and eleven quarterings in his arms; the rest of the genealogical tree belonging to the family having been lost through the injuries of time.

The Baron was one of the most powerful lords in Westphalia, for his castle had not only a gate, but even windows, and his great hall was hung with tapestry. He used to hunt with his mastiffs and spaniels instead of greyhounds; his groom served him for huntsman; and the parson of the parish officiated as his grand almoner. He was called "My Lord" by all his people, and he never told a story but everyone laughed at it.

My Lady Baroness, who weighed three hundred and fifty pounds, consequently was a person of no small consideration; and then she did the honors of the house with a dignity that commanded universal respect. Her daughter was about seventeen years of age, fresh–colored, comely, plump, and desirable. The Baron's son seemed to be a youth in every respect worthy of the father he sprung from. Pangloss, the preceptor, was the oracle of the family, and little Candide listened to his instructions with all the simplicity natural to his age and disposition.

Master Pangloss taught the metaphysico–theologo–cosmolonigology.He could prove to admiration that there is no effect without a cause; and, that in this best of all possible worlds, the Baron's castle was the most magnificent of all castles, and My Lady the best of all possible baronesses.

"It is demonstrable," said he, "that things cannot be otherwise than as they are; for as all things have been created for some end, they must necessarily be created for the best end. Observe, for instance, the nose is formed for spectacles, therefore we wear spectacles. The legs are visibly designed for stockings, accordingly we wear stockings. Stones were made to be hewn and to construct castles, therefore My Lord has a magnificent castle; for the greatest baron in the province ought to be the best lodged. Swine were intended to be eaten, therefore we eat pork all the year round: and they, who assert that everything is right, do not express themselves correctly; they should say that everything is best."

Candide listened attentively and believed implicitly, for he thought Miss Cunegund excessively handsome, though he never had the courage to tell her so. He concluded that next to the happiness of being Baron of Thunder–ten–tronckh, the next was that of being Miss Cunegund, the next that of seeing her every day, and the last that of hearing the doctrine of Master Pangloss, the greatest philosopher of the whole province, and consequently of the whole world.

One day when Miss Cunegund went to take a walk in a little neighboring wood which was called a park, she saw, through the bushes, the sage Doctor Pangloss giving a lecture in experimental philosophy to her mother's chambermaid, a little brown wench, very pretty, and very tractable. As Miss Cunegund had a great disposition for the sciences, she observed with the utmost attention the experiments which were repeated before her eyes; she perfectly well understood the force of the doctor's reasoning upon causes and effects. She retired greatly flurried, quite pensive and filled with the desire of knowledge, imagining that she might be a sufficing reason for young Candide, and he for her.

On her way back she happened to meet the young man; she blushed, he blushed also; she wished him a good morning in a flattering tone, he returned the salute, without knowing what he said. The next day, as they were rising from dinner, Cunegund and Candide slipped behind the screen. The miss dropped her handkerchief, the young man picked it up. She innocently took hold of his hand, and he as innocently kissed hers with a warmth, a sensibility, a grace–all very particular; their lips met; their eyes sparkled; their knees trembled; their hands strayed. The Baron chanced to come by; he beheld the cause and effect, and, without hesitation, saluted Candide with some notable kicks on the breech and drove him out of doors. The lovely Miss Cunegund fainted away, and, as soon as she came to herself, the Baroness boxed her ears. Thus a general consternation was spread over this most magnificent and most agreeable of all possible castles.

CHAPTER 2

What Befell Candide among the Bulgarians

Candide, thus driven out of this terrestrial paradise, rambled a long time without knowing where he went; sometimes he raised his eyes, all bedewed with tears, towards heaven, and sometimes he cast a melancholy look towards the magnificent castle, where dwelt the fairest of young baronesses. He laid himself down to sleep in a furrow, heartbroken, and supperless. The snow fell in great flakes, and, in the morning when he awoke, he was almost frozen to death; however, he made shift to crawl to the next town, which was called Wald–berghoff-trarbkdikdorff, without a penny in his pocket, and half dead with hunger and fatigue. He took up his stand at the door of an inn. He had not been long there before two men dressed in blue fixed their eyes steadfastly upon him.

"Faith, comrade," said one of them to the other, "yonder is a well made young fellow and of the right size." Upon which they made up to Candide and with the greatest civility and politeness invited him to dine with them.

"Gentlemen," replied Candide, with a most engaging modesty, you do me much honor, but upon my word I have no money."

"Money, sir!" said one of the blues to him, "young persons of your appearance and merit never pay anything; why, are not you five feet five inches high?"

"Yes, gentlemen, that is really my size," replied he, with a low bow.

"Come then, sir, sit down along with us; we will not only pay your reckoning, but will never suffer such a clever young fellow as you to want money. Men were born to assist one another."

"You are perfectly right, gentlemen," said Candide, "this is precisely the doctrine of Master Pangloss; and I am convinced that everything is for the best."

His generous companions next entreated him to accept of a few crowns, which he readily complied with, at the same time offering them his note for the payment, which they refused, and sat down to table.

"Have you not a great affection for –"

"O yes! I have a great affection for the lovely Miss Cunegund."

"Maybe so," replied one of the blues, "but that is not the question! We ask you whether you have not a great affection for the King of the Bulgarians?"

"For the King of the Bulgarians?" said Candide. "Oh, Lord! not at all, why I never saw him in my life."

"Is it possible? Oh, he is a most charming king! Come, we must drink his health."

"With all my heart, gentlemen," said Candide, and off he tossed his glass.

"Bravo!" cried the blues; "you are now the support, the defender, the hero of the Bulgarians; your fortune is made; you are in the high road to glory."

So saying, they handcuffed him, and carried him away to the regiment. There he was made to wheel about to the right, to the left, to draw his rammer, to return his rammer, to present, to fire, to march, and they gave him thirty blows with a cane; the next day he performed his exercise a little better, and they gave him but twenty; the day following he came off with ten, and was looked upon as a young fellow of surprising genius by all his comrades.

Candide was struck with amazement, and could not for the soul of him conceive how he came to be a hero. One fine spring morning, he took it into his head to take a walk, and he marched straight forward, conceiving it to be a privilege of the human species, as well as of the brute creation, to make use of their legs how and when they pleased. He had not gone above two leagues when he was overtaken by four other heroes, six feet high, who bound him neck and heels, and carried him to a dungeon. A courtmartial sat upon him, and he was asked which he liked better, to run the gauntlet six and thirty times through the whole regiment, or to have his brains blown out with a dozen musket–balls?

In vain did he remonstrate to them that the human will is free, and that he chose neither; they obliged him to make a choice, and he determined, in virtue of that divine gift called free will, to run the gauntlet six and thirty times.

He had gone through his discipline twice, and the regiment being composed of 2,000 men, they composed for him exactly 4,000 strokes, which laid bare all his muscles and nerves from the nape of his neck to his stern. As they were preparing to make him set out the third time our young hero, unable to support it any longer, begged as a favor that they would be so obliging as to shoot him through the head; the favor being granted, a bandage was tied over his eyes, and he was made to kneel down.

At that very instant, His Bulgarian Majesty happening to pass by made a stop, and inquired into the delinquent's crime, and being a prince of great penetration, he found, from what he heard of Candide, that he was a young metaphysician, entirely ignorant of the world; and therefore, out of his great clemency, he condescended to pardon him, for which his name will be celebrated in every journal, and in every age. A skillful surgeon made a cure of the flagellated Candide in three weeks by means of emollient unguents prescribed by Dioscorides. His sores were now skimmed over and he was able to march, when the King of the Bulgarians gave battle to the King of the Abares.

CHAPTER 3

How Candide Escaped from the Bulgarians and What Befell Him Afterward

Never was anything so gallant, so well accoutred, so brilliant, and so finely disposed as the two armies. The trumpets, fifes, hautboys, drums, and cannon made such harmony as never was heard in Hell itself. The entertainment began by a discharge of cannon, which, in the twinkling of an eye, laid flat about 6,000 men on each side. The musket bullets swept away, out of the best of all possible worlds, nine or ten thousand scoundrels that infested its surface. The bayonet was next the sufficient reason of the deaths of several thousands. The whole might amount to thirty thousand souls. Candide trembled like a philosopher, and concealed himself as well as he could during this heroic butchery.

At length, while the two kings were causing Te Deums to be sung in their camps, Candide took a resolution to go and reason somewhere else upon causes and effects. After passing over heaps of dead or dying men, the first place he came to was a neighboring village, in the Abarian territories, which had been burned to the ground by the Bulgarians, agreeably to the laws of war. Here lay a number of old men covered with wounds, who beheld their wives dying with their throats cut, and hugging their children to their breasts, all stained with blood. There several young virgins, whose bodies had been ripped open, after they had satisfied the natural necessities of the Bulgarian heroes, breathed their last; while others, half–burned in the flames, begged to be dispatched out of the world. The ground about them was covered with the brains, arms, and legs of dead men.

Candide made all the haste he could to another village, which belonged to the Bulgarians, and there he found the heroic Abares had enacted the same tragedy. Thence continuing to walk over palpitating limbs, or through ruined buildings, at length he arrived beyond the theater of war, with a little provision in his budget, and Miss Cunegund's image in his heart. When he arrived in Holland his provision failed him; but having heard that the inhabitants of that country were all rich and Christians, he made himself sure of being treated by them in the same manner as the Baron's castle, before he had been driven thence through the power of Miss Cunegund's bright eyes.

He asked charity of several grave–looking people, who one and all answered him, that if he continued to follow this trade they would have him sent to the house of correction, where he should be taught to get his bread.

He next addressed himself to a person who had just come from haranguing a numerous assembly for a whole hour on the subject of charity. The orator, squinting at him under his broadbrimmed hat, asked him sternly, what brought him thither and whether he was for the good old cause?

"Sir," said Candide, in a submissive manner, "I conceive there can be no effect without a cause; everything is necessarily concatenated and arranged for the best. It was necessary that I should be banished from the presence of Miss Cunegund; that I should afterwards run the gauntlet; and it is necessary I should beg my bread, till I am able to get it. All this could not have been otherwise."

"Hark ye, friend," said the orator, "do you hold the Pope to be Antichrist?"

"Truly, I never heard anything about it," said Candide, "but whether he is or not, I am in want of something to eat."

"Thou deservest not to eat or to drink," replied the orator, "wretch, monster, that thou art! hence! avoid my sight, nor ever come near me again while thou livest."

The orator's wife happened to put her head out of the window at that instant, when, seeing a man who doubted whether the Pope was Antichrist, she discharged upon his head a utensil full of water. Good heavens, to what excess does religious zeal transport womankind!

A man who had never been christened, an honest Anabaptist named James, was witness to the cruel and ignominious treatment showed to one of his brethren, to a rational, two–footed, unfledged being. Moved with pity he carried him to his own house, caused him to be cleaned, gave him meat and drink, and made him a present of two florins, at the same time proposing to instruct him in his own trade of weaving Persian silks, which are fabricated in Holland.

Candide, penetrated with so much goodness, threw himself at his feet, crying, "Now I am convinced that my Master Pangloss told me truth when he said that everything was for the best in this world; for I am infinitely more affected with your extraordinary generosity than with the inhumanity of that gentleman in the black cloak and his wife."

CHAPTER 4

How Candide Found His Old Master Pangloss Again and What Happened to Him

The next day, as Candide was walking out, he met a beggar all covered with scabs, his eyes sunk in his head, the end of his nose eaten off, his mouth drawn on one side, his teeth as black as a cloak, snuffling and coughing most violently, and every time he attempted to spit out dropped a tooth.

Candide, divided between compassion and horror, but giving way to the former, bestowed on this shocking figure the two florins which the honest Anabaptist, James, had just before given to him. The specter looked at him very earnestly, shed tears and threw his arms about his neck. Candide started back aghast.

"Alas!" said the one wretch to the other, "don't you know dear Pangloss?"

"What do I hear? Is it you, my dear master! you I behold in this piteous plight? What dreadful misfortune has befallen you? What has made you leave the most magnificent and delightful of all castles?What has become of Miss Cunegund, the mirror of young ladies, and Nature's masterpiece?"

"Oh, Lord!" cried Pangloss, "I am so weak I cannot stand," upon which Candide instantly led him to the Anabaptist's stable, and procured him something to eat.

As soon as Pangloss had a little refreshed himself, Candide began to repeat his inquiries concerning Miss Cunegund.

"She is dead," replied the other.

"Dead!" cried Candide, and immediately fainted away; his friend restored him by the help of a little bad vinegar, which he found by chance in the stable.

Candide opened his eyes, and again repeated: "Dead! is Miss Cunegund dead? Ah, where is the best of worlds now? But of what illness did she die? Was it of grief on seeing her father kick me out of his magnificent castle?"

"No," replied Pangloss, "her body was ripped open by the Bulgarian soldiers, after they had subjected her to as much cruelty as a damsel could survive; they knocked the Baron, her father, on the head for attempting to defend her; My Lady, her mother, was cut in pieces; my poor pupil was served just in the same manner as his sister; and as for the castle, they have not left one stone upon another; they have destroyed all the ducks, and sheep, the barns, and the trees; but we have had our revenge, for the Abares have done the very same thing in a neighboring barony, which belonged to a Bulgarian lord."

At hearing this, Candide fainted away a second time, but, not withstanding, having come to himself again, he said all that it became him to say; he inquired into the cause and effect, as well as into the sufficing reason that had reduced Pangloss to so miserable a condition.

"Alas," replied the preceptor, "it was love; love, the comfort of the human species; love, the preserver of the universe; the soul of all sensible beings; love! tender love!"

"Alas," cried Candide, "I have had some knowledge of love myself, this sovereign of hearts, this soul of souls; yet it never cost me more than a kiss and twenty kicks on the backside. But how could this beautiful cause produce in you so hideous an effect?"

Pangloss made answer in these terms:

"O my dear Candide, you must remember Pacquette, that pretty wench, who waited on our noble Baroness; in her arms I tasted the pleasures of Paradise, which produced these Hell torments with which you see me devoured. She was infected with an ailment, and perhaps has since died of it; she received this present of a learned Franciscan, who derived it from the fountainhead; he was indebted for it to an old countess, who had it of a captain of horse, who had it of a marchioness, who had it of a page, the page had it of a Jesuit, who, during his novitiate, had it in a direct line from one of the fellow adventurers of Christopher Columbus; for my part I shall give it to nobody, I am a dying man."

"O sage Pangloss," cried Candide, "what a strange genealogy is this!Is not the devil the root of it?"

"Not at all," replied the great man, "it was a thing unavoidable, a necessary ingredient in the best of worlds; for if Columbus had not caught in an island in America this disease, which contaminates the source of generation, and frequently impedes propagation itself, and is evidently opposed to the great end of nature, we should have had neither chocolate nor cochineal. It is also to be observed, that, even to the present time, in this continent of ours, this malady, like our religious controversies, is peculiar to ourselves.The Turks, the Indians, the Persians, the Chinese, the Siamese, and the Japanese are entirely unacquainted with it; but there is a sufficing reason for them to know it in a few centuries. In the meantime, it is making prodigious havoc among us, especially in those armies composed of well disciplined hirelings, who determine the fate of nations; for we may safely affirm, that, when an army of thirty thousand men engages another equal in size, there are about twenty thousand infected with syphilis on each side."

"Very surprising, indeed," said Candide, "but you must get cured."

"Lord help me, how can I?" said Pangloss. "My dear friend, I have not a penny in the world; and you know one cannot be bled or have an enema without money."

This last speech had its effect on Candide; he flew to the charitable Anabaptist, James; he flung himself at his feet, and gave him so striking a picture of the miserable condition of his friend that the good man without any further hesitation agreed to take Dr.Pangloss into his house, and to pay for his cure. The cure was effected with only the loss of one eye and an ear. As be wrote a good hand, and understood accounts tolerably well, the Anabaptist made him his bookkeeper. At the expiration of two months, being obliged by some mercantile affairs to go to Lisbon he took the two philosophers with him in the same ship; Pangloss, during the course of the voyage, explained to him how everything was so constituted that it could not be better. James did not quite agree with him on this point.

"Men," said he "must, in some things, have deviated from their original innocence; for they were not born wolves, and yet they worry one another like those beasts of prey. God never gave them twenty–four pounders nor bayonets, and yet they have made cannon and bayonets to destroy one another. To this account I might add not only bankruptcies, but the law which seizes on the effects of bankrupts, only to cheat the creditors."

"All this was indispensably necessary," replied the one–eyed doctor, "for private misfortunes are public benefits; so that the more private misfortunes there are, the greater is the general good."

While he was arguing in this manner, the sky was overcast, the winds blew from the four quarters of the compass, and the ship was assailed by a most terrible tempest, within sight of the port of Lisbon.

CHAPTER 5

A Tempest, a Shipwreck, an Earthquake, and What Else Befell Dr. Pangloss, Candide, and James, the Anabaptist

One half of the passengers, weakened and half–dead with the inconceivable anxiety and sickness which the rolling of a vessel at sea occasions through the whole human frame, were lost to all sense of the danger that surrounded them. The others made loud outcries, or betook themselves to their prayers; the sails were blown into shreds, and the masts were brought by the board. The vessel was a total wreck. Everyone was busily employed, but nobody could be either heard or obeyed. The Anabaptist, being upon deck, lent a helping hand as well as the rest, when a brutish sailor gave him a blow and laid him speechless; but, not withstanding, with the violence of the blow the tar himself tumbled headforemost overboard, and fell upon a piece of the broken mast, which he immediately grasped.

Honest James, forgetting the injury he had so lately received from him, flew to his assistance, and, with great difficulty, hauled him in again, but, not withstanding, in the attempt, was, by a sudden jerk of the ship, thrown overboard himself, in sight of the very fellow whom he had risked his life to save and who took not the least notice of him in this distress. Candide, who beheld all that passed and saw his benefactor one moment rising above water, and the next swallowed up by the merciless waves, was preparing to jump after him, but was prevented by the philosopher Pangloss, who demonstrated to him that the roadstead of Lisbon had been made on purpose for the Anabaptist to be drowned there. While he was proving his argument a priori, the ship foundered, and the whole crew perished, except Pangloss, Candide, and the sailor who had been the means of drowning the good Anabaptist.The villain swam ashore; but Pangloss and Candide reached the land upon a plank.

As soon as they had recovered from their surprise and fatigue they walked towards Lisbon; with what little money they had left they thought to save themselves from starving after having escaped drowning.

Scarcely had they ceased to lament the loss of their benefactor and set foot in the city, when they perceived that the earth trembled under their feet, and the sea, swelling and foaming in the harbor, was dashing in pieces the vessels that were riding at anchor. Large sheets of flames and cinders covered the streets and public places; the houses tottered, and were tumbled topsy–turvy even to their foundations, which were themselves destroyed, and thirty thousand inhabitants of both sexes, young and old, were buried beneath the ruins.

The sailor, whistling and swearing, cried, "Damn it, there's something to be got here."

"What can be the sufficing reason of this phenomenon?" said Pangloss.

"It is certainly the day of judgment," said Candide.

The sailor, defying death in the pursuit of plunder, rushed into the midst of the ruin, where he found some money, with which he got drunk, and, after he had slept himself sober he purchased the favors of the first good–natured wench that came in his way, amidst the ruins of demolished houses and the groans of half–buried and expiring persons.

Pangloss pulled him by the sleeve. "Friend," said he, "this is not right, you trespass against the universal reason, and have mistaken your time."

"Death and zounds!" answered the other, "I am a sailor and was born at Batavia, and have trampled four times upon the crucifix in as many voyages to Japan; you have come to a good hand with your universal reason."

In the meantime, Candide, who had been wounded by some pieces of stone that fell from the houses, lay stretched in the street, almost covered with rubbish.

"For God's sake," said he to Pangloss, "get me a little wine and oil! I am dying."

"This concussion of the earth is no new thing," said Pangloss, "the city of Lima in South America experienced the same last year; the same cause, the same effects; there is certainly a train of sulphur all the way underground from Lima to Lisbon."

"Nothing is more probable," said Candide; "but for the love of God a little oil and wine."

"Probable!" replied the philosopher, "I maintain that the thing is demonstrable."

Candide fainted away, and Pangloss fetched him some water from a neighboring spring. The next day, in searching among the ruins, they found some eatables with which they repaired their exhausted strength.After this they assisted the inhabitants in relieving the distressed and wounded. Some, whom they had humanely assisted, gave them as good a dinner as could be expected under such terrible circumstances. The repast, indeed, was mournful, and the company moistened their bread with their tears; but Pangloss endeavored to comfort them under this affliction by affirming that things could not be otherwise that they were.

"For," said he, "all this is for the very best end, for if there is a volcano at Lisbon it could be in no other spot; and it is impossible but things should be as they are, for everything is for the best."

By the side of the preceptor sat a little man dressed in black, who was one of the familiars of the Inquisition. This person, taking him up with great complaisance, said, "Possibly, my good sir, you do not believe in original sin; for, if everything is best, there could have been no such thing as the fall or punishment of man."

Your Excellency will pardon me," answered Pangloss, still more politely; "for the fall of man and the curse consequent thereupon necessarily entered into the system of the best of worlds."

"That is as much as to say, sir," rejoined the familiar, "you do not believe in free will."

"Your Excellency will be so good as to excuse me," said Pangloss, "free will is consistent with absolute necessity; for it was necessary we should be free, for in that the will –"

Pangloss was in the midst of his proposition, when the familiar beckoned to his attendant to help him to a glass of port wine.

CHAPTER 6

How the Portuguese Made a Superb Auto–De–Fe to Prevent Any Future Earthquakes, and How Candide Underwent Public Flagellation

After the earthquake, which had destroyed three–fourths of the city of Lisbon, the sages of that country could think of no means more effectual to preserve the kingdom from utter ruin than to entertain the people with an auto–da–fe, it having been decided by the University of Coimbra, that the burning of a few people alive by a slow fire, and with great ceremony, is an infallible preventive of earthquakes.

In consequence thereof they had seized on a Biscayan for marrying his godmother, and on two Portuguese for taking out the bacon of a larded pullet they were eating; after dinner they came and secured Dr.Pangloss, and his pupil Candide, the one for speaking his mind, and the other for seeming to approve what he had said. They were conducted to separate apartments, extremely cool, where they were never incommoded with the sun. Eight days afterwards they were each dressed in a sanbenito, and their heads were adorned with paper mitres. The mitre and sanbenito worn by Candide were painted with flames reversed and with devils that had neither tails nor claws; but Dr. Pangloss's devils had both tails and claws, and his flames were upright. In these habits they marched in procession, and heard a very pathetic sermon, which was followed by an anthem, accompanied by bagpipes. Candide was flogged to some tune, while the anthem was being sung; the Biscayan and the two men who would not eat bacon were burned, and Pangloss was hanged, which is not a common custom at these solemnities. The same day there was another earthquake, which made most dreadful havoc.

Candide, amazed, terrified, confounded, astonished, all bloody, and trembling from head to foot, said to himself, "If this is the best of all possible worlds, what are the others? If I had only been whipped, I could have put up with it, as I did among the Bulgarians; but, not withstanding, oh my dear Pangloss! my beloved master! thou greatest of philosophers! that ever I should live to see thee hanged, without knowing for what! O my dear Anabaptist, thou best of men, that it should be thy fate to be drowned in the very harbor! O Miss Cunegund, you mirror of young ladies! that it should be your fate to have your body ripped open!"

He was making the best of his way from the place where he had been preached to, whipped, absolved and blessed, when he was accosted by an old woman, who said to him, "Take courage, child, and follow me."

CHAPTER 7

How the Old Woman Took Care Of Candide, and How He Found the Object of His Love

Candide followed the old woman, though without taking courage, to a decayed house, where she gave him a pot of pomatum to anoint his sores, showed him a very neat bed, with a suit of clothes hanging by it; and set victuals and drink before him.

"There," said she, "eat, drink, and sleep, and may Our Lady of Atocha, and the great St. Anthony of Padua, and the illustrious St.James of Compostella, take you under their protection. I shall be back tomorrow."

Candide, struck with amazement at what he had seen, at what he had suffered, and still more with the charity of the old woman, would have shown his acknowledgment by kissing her hand.

"It is not my hand you ought to kiss," said the old woman. "I shall be back tomorrow. Anoint your back, eat, and take your rest."

Candide, notwithstanding so many disasters, ate and slept. The next morning, the old woman brought him his breakfast; examined his back, and rubbed it herself with another ointment. She returned at the proper time, and brought him his dinner; and at night, she visited him again with his supper. The next day she observed the same ceremonies.

"Who are you?" said Candide to her. "Who has inspired you with so much goodness? What return can I make you for this charitable assistance?"

The good old beldame kept a profound silence. In the evening she returned, but without his supper.

"Come along with me," said she, "but do not speak a word."

She took him by the arm, and walked with him about a quarter of a mile into the country, till they came to a lonely house surrounded with moats and gardens. The old conductress knocked at a little door, which was immediately opened, and she showed him up a pair of back stairs, into a small, but richly furnished apartment. There she made him sit down on a brocaded sofa, shut the door upon him, and left him. Candide thought himself in a trance; he looked upon his whole life, hitherto, as a frightful dream, and the present moment as a very agreeable one.

The old woman soon returned, supporting, with great difficulty, a young lady, who appeared scarce able to stand. She was of a majestic mien and stature, her dress was rich, and glittering with diamonds, and her face was covered with a veil.

"Take off that veil," said the old woman to Candide.

The young man approached, and, with a trembling hand, took off her veil. What a happy moment! What surprise! He thought he beheld Miss Cunegund; he did behold her – it was she herself. His strength failed him, he could not utter a word, he fell at her feet. Cunegund fainted upon the sofa. The old woman bedewed them with spirits; they recovered – they began to speak. At first they could express themselves only in broken accents; their questions and answers were alternately interrupted with sighs, tears, and exclamations. The old woman desired them to make less noise, and after this prudent admonition left them together.

"Good heavens!" cried Candide, "is it you? Is it Miss Cunegund I behold, and alive? Do I find you again in Portugal? then you have not been ravished? they did not rip open your body, as the philosopher Pangloss informed me?"

"Indeed but they did," replied Miss Cunegund; "but these two accidents do not always prove mortal."

"But were your father and mother killed?"

"Alas!" answered she, "it is but too true!" and she wept.

"And your brother?"

"And my brother also."

"And how came you into Portugal? And how did you know of my being here? And by what strange adventure did you contrive to have me brought into this house? And how –"

"I will tell you all," replied the lady, "but first you must acquaint me with all that has befallen you since the innocent kiss you gave me, and the rude kicking you received in consequence of it."

Candide, with the greatest submission, prepared to obey the commands of his fair mistress; and though he was still filled with amazement, though his voice was low and tremulous, though his back pained him, yet he gave her a most ingenuous account of everything that had befallen him, since the moment of their separation. Cunegund, with her eyes uplifted to heaven, shed tears when he related the death of the good Anabaptist, James, and of Pangloss; after which she thus related her adventures to Candide, who lost not one syllable she uttered, and seemed to devour her with his eyes all the time she was speaking.

CHAPTER 8

Cunegund's Story

I was in bed, and fast asleep, when it pleased Heaven to send the Bulgarians to our delightful castle of Thunder–ten–tronckh, where they murdered my father and brother, and cut my mother in pieces. A tall Bulgarian soldier, six feet high, perceiving that I had fainted away at this sight, attempted to ravish me; the operation brought me to my senses. I cried, I struggled, I bit, I scratched, I would have torn the tall Bulgarian's eyes out, not knowing that what had happened at my father's castle was a customary thing. The brutal soldier, enraged at my resistance, gave me a wound in my left leg with his hanger, the mark of which I still carry."

"Methinks I long to see it," said Candide, with all imaginable simplicity.

"You shall," said Cunegund, "but let me proceed."

"Pray do," replied Candide.

She continued. "A Bulgarian captain came in, and saw me weltering in my blood, and the soldier still as busy as if no one had been present.The officer, enraged at the fellow's want of respect to him, killed him with one stroke of his sabre as he lay upon me. This captain took care of me, had me cured, and carried me as a prisoner of war to his quarters. I washed what little linen he possessed, and cooked his victuals: he was very fond of me, that was certain; neither can I deny that he was well made, and had a soft, white skin, but he was very stupid, and knew nothing of philosophy: it might plainly be perceived that he had not been educated under Dr. Pangloss. In three months, having gambled away all his money, and having grown tired of me, he sold me to a Jew, named Don Issachar, who traded in Holland and Portugal, and was passionately fond of women. This Jew showed me great kindness, in hopes of gaining my favors; but he never could prevail on me to yield. A modest woman may be once ravished; but her virtue is greatly strengthened thereby. In order to make sure of me, he brought me to this country house you now see. I had hitherto believed that nothing could equal the beauty of the castle of Thunder–ten–tronckh; but I found I was mistaken.

"The Grand Inquisitor saw me one day at Mass, ogled me all the time of service, and when it was over, sent to let me know he wanted to speak with me about some private business. I was conducted to his palace, where I told him all my story; he represented to me how much it was beneath a person of my birth to belong to a circumcised Israelite. He caused a proposal to be made to Don Issachar, that he should resign me to His Lordship. Don Issachar, being the court banker and a man of credit, was not easy to be prevailed upon. His Lordship threatened him with an auto–da–fe; in short, my Jew was frightened into a compromise, and it was agreed between them, that the house and myself should belong to both in common; that the Jew should have Monday, Wednesday, and the Sabbath to himself; and the Inquisitor the other four days of the week. This agreement has subsisted almost six months; but not without several contests, whether the space from Saturday night to Sunday morning belonged to the old or the new law.For my part, I have hitherto withstood them both, and truly I believe this is the very reason why they are both so fond of me.

"At length to turn aside the scourge of earthquakes, and to intimidate Don Issachar, My Lord Inquisitor was pleased to celebrate an auto–da–fe. He did me the honor to invite me to the ceremony. I had a very good seat; and refreshments of all kinds were offered the ladies between Mass and the execution. I was dreadfully shocked at the burning of the two Jews, and the honest Biscayan who married his godmother; but how great was my surprise, my consternation, and concern, when I beheld a figure so like Pangloss, dressed in a sanbenito and mitre! I rubbed my eyes, I looked at him attentively.I saw him hanged, and I fainted away: scarce had I recovered my senses, when I saw you stripped of clothing; this was the height of horror, grief, and despair. I must confess to you for a truth, that your skin is whiter and more blooming than that of the Bulgarian captain. This spectacle worked me up to a pitch of distraction. I screamed out, and would have said, 'Hold, barbarians!' but my voice failed me; and indeed my cries would have signified nothing. After you had been severely whipped, I said to myself, 'How is it possible that the lovely Candide and the sage Pangloss should be at Lisbon, the one to receive a hundred lashes, and the other to be hanged by order of My Lord Inquisitor, of whom I am so great a favorite? Pangloss deceived me most cruelly, in saying that everything is for the best.'

"Thus agitated and perplexed, now distracted and lost, now half dead with grief, I revolved in my mind the murder of my father, mother, and brother, committed before my eyes; the insolence of the rascally Bulgarian soldier; the wound he gave me in the groin; my servitude; my being a cook–wench to my Bulgarian captain; my subjection to the hateful Jew, and my cruel Inquisitor; the hanging of Doctor Pangloss; the Miserere sung while you were being whipped; and particularly the kiss I gave you behind the screen, the last day I ever beheld you. I returned thanks to God for having brought you to the place where I was, after so many trials. I charged the old woman who attends me to bring you hither as soon as was convenient. She has punctually executed my orders, and I now enjoy the inexpressible satisfaction of seeing you, hearing you, and speaking to you. But you must certainly be half-dead with hunger; I myself have a great inclination to eat, and so let us sit down to supper."

Upon this the two lovers immediately placed themselves at table, and, after having supped, they returned to seat themselves again on the magnificent sofa already mentioned, where they were in amorous dalliance, when Senor Don Issachar, one of the masters of the house, entered unexpectedly; it was the Sabbath day, and he came to enjoy his privilege, and sigh forth his passion at the feet of the fair Cunegund.

CHAPTER 9

What Happened to Cunegund, Candide, the Grand Inquisitor, and the Jew

This same Issachar was the most choleric little Hebrew that had ever been in Israel since the captivity of Babylon.

"What," said he, "thou Galilean slut? The Inquisitor was not enough for thee, but this rascal must come in for a share with me?"

In uttering these words, he drew out a long poniard, which he always carried about him, and never dreaming that his adversary had any arms, he attacked him most furiously; but our honest Westphalian had received from the old woman a handsome sword with the suit of clothes.Candide drew his rapier, and though he was very gentle and sweet–tempered, he laid the Israelite dead on the floor at the fair Cunegund's feet.

"Holy Virgin!" cried she, "what will become of us? A man killed in my apartment! If the peace–officers come, we are undone."

"Had not Pangloss been hanged," replied Candide, "he would have given us most excellent advice, in this emergency; for he was a profound philosopher. But, since he is not here, let us consult the old woman."

She was very sensible, and was beginning to give her advice, when another door opened on a sudden. It was now one o'clock in the morning, and of course the beginning of Sunday, which, by agreement, fell to the lot of My Lord Inquisitor. Entering he discovered the flagellated Candide with his drawn sword in his hand, a dead body stretched on the floor, Cunegund frightened out of her wits, and the old woman giving advice.

At that very moment, a sudden thought came into Candide's head."If this holy man," thought he, "should call assistance, I shall most undoubtedly be consigned to the flames, and Miss Cunegund may perhaps meet with no better treatment: besides, he was the cause of my being so cruelly whipped; he is my rival; and as I have now begun to dip my hands in blood, I will kill away, for there is no time to hesitate."

This whole train of reasoning was clear and instantaneous; so that, without giving time to the Inquisitor to recover from his surprise, he ran him through the body, and laid him by the side of the Jew.

"Here's another fine piece of work!" cried Cunegund. "Now there can be no mercy for us, we are excommunicated; our last hour is come. But how could you, who are of so mild a temper, despatch a Jew and an Inquisitor in two minutes' time?"

"Beautiful maiden," answered Candide, "when a man is in love, is jealous, and has been flogged by the Inquisition, he becomes lost to all reflection."

The old woman then put in her word:

"There are three Andalusian horses in the stable, with as many bridles and saddles; let the brave Candide get them ready. Madam has a parcel of moidores and jewels, let us mount immediately, though I have lost one buttock; let us set out for Cadiz; it is the finest weather in the world, and there is great pleasure in traveling in the cool of the night."

Candide, without any further hesitation, saddled the three horses; and Miss Cunegund, the old woman, and he, set out, and traveled thirty miles without once halting. While they were making the best of their way, the Holy Brotherhood entered the house. My Lord, the Inquisitor, was interred in a magnificent manner, and Master Issachar's body was thrown upon a dunghill.

Candide, Cunegund, and the old woman, had by this time reached the little town of Avacena, in the midst of the mountains of Sierra Morena, and were engaged in the following conversation in an inn, where they had taken up their quarters.

CHAPTER 10

In What Distress Candide, Cunegund, and the Old Woman Arrive at Cadiz, and Of Their Embarkation

Who could it be that has robbed me of my moidores and jewels?" exclaimed Miss Cunegund, all bathed in tears. "How shall we live? What shall we do? Where shall I find Inquisitors and Jews who can give me more?"

"Alas!" said the old woman, "I have a shrewd suspicion of a reverend Franciscan father, who lay last night in the same inn with us at Badajoz. God forbid I should condemn any one wrongfully, but he came into our room twice, and he set off in the morning long before us."

"Alas!" said Candide, "Pangloss has often demonstrated to me that the goods of this world are common to all men, and that everyone has an equal right to the enjoyment of them; but, not withstanding, according to these principles, the Franciscan ought to have left us enough to carry us to the end of our journey. Have you nothing at all left, my dear Miss Cunegund?"

"Not a maravedi," replied she.

"What is to be done then?" said Candide.

"Sell one of the horses," replied the old woman. "I will get up behind Miss Cunegund, though I have only one buttock to ride on, and we shall reach Cadiz."

In the same inn there was a Benedictine friar, who bought the horse very cheap. Candide, Cunegund, and the old woman, after passing through Lucina, Chellas, and Letrixa, arrived at length at Cadiz. A fleet was then getting ready, and troops were assembling in order to induce the reverend fathers, Jesuits of Paraguay, who were accused of having excited one of the Indian tribes in the neighborhood of the town of the Holy Sacrament, to revolt against the Kings of Spain and Portugal.

Candide, having been in the Bulgarian service, performed the military exercise of that nation before the general of this little army with so intrepid an air, and with such agility and expedition, that he received the command of a company of foot. Being now made a captain, he embarked with Miss Cunegund, the old woman, two valets, and the two Andalusian horses, which had belonged to the Grand Inquisitor of Portugal.

During their voyage they amused themselves with many profound reasonings on poor Pangloss's philosophy.

"We are now going into another world, and surely it must be there that everything is for the best; for I must confess that we have had some little reason to complain of what passes in ours, both as to the physical and moral part. Though I have a sincere love for you," said Miss Cunegund, "yet I still shudder at the reflection of what I have seen and experienced."

"All will be well," replied Candide, "the sea of this new world is already better than our European seas: it is smoother, and the winds blow more regularly."

"God grant it," said Cunegund, "but I have met with such terrible treatment in this world that I have almost lost all hopes of a better one."

"What murmuring and complaining is here indeed!" cried the old woman. "If you had suffered half what I have, there might be some reason for it."

Miss Cunegund could scarce refrain from laughing at the good old woman, and thought it droll enough to pretend to a greater share of misfortunes than her own.

"Alas! my good dame," said she, "unless you had been ravished by two Bulgarians, had received two deep wounds in your belly, had seen two of your own castles demolished, had lost two fathers, and two mothers, and seen both of them barbarously murdered before your eyes, and to sum up all, had two lovers whipped at an auto–da–fe, I cannot see how you could be more unfortunate than I. Add to this, though born a baroness, and bearing seventy–two quarterings, I have been reduced to the station of a cook–wench."

"Miss," replied the old woman, "you do not know my family as yet; but if I were to show you my posteriors, you would not talk in this manner, but suspend your judgment." This speech raised a high curiosity in Candide and Cunegund; and the old woman continued as follows.

CHAPTER 11

The History of the Old Woman

I have not always been blear–eyed. My nose did not always touch my chin; nor was I always a servant. You must know that I am the daughter of Pope Urban X, and of the Princess of Palestrina. To the age of fourteen I was brought up in a castle, compared with which all the castles of the German barons would not have been fit for stabling, and one of my robes would have bought half the province of Westphalia. I grew up, and improved in beauty, wit, and every graceful accomplishment; and in the midst of pleasures, homage, and the highest expectations. I already began to inspire the men with love. My breast began to take its right form, and such a breast! white, firm, and formed like that of the Venus de' Medici; my eyebrows were as black as jet, and as for my eyes, they darted flames and eclipsed the luster of the stars, as I was told by the poets of our part of the world. My maids, when they dressed and undressed me, used to fall into an ecstasy in viewing me before and behind; and all the men longed to be in their places.

"I was contracted in marriage to a sovereign prince of Massa Carrara. Such a prince! as handsome as myself, sweet–tempered, agreeable, witty, and in love with me over head and ears. I loved him, too, as our sex generally do for the first time, with rapture, transport, and idolatry. The nuptials were prepared with surprising pomp and magnificence; the ceremony was attended with feasts, carousals, and burlesques: all Italy composed sonnets in my praise, though not one of them was tolerable.

"I was on the point of reaching the summit of bliss, when an old marchioness, who had been mistress to the Prince, my husband, invited him to drink chocolate. In less than two hours after he returned from the visit, he died of most terrible convulsions.

"But this is a mere trifle. My mother, distracted to the highest degree, and yet less afflicted than I, determined to absent herself for some time from so fatal a place. As she had a very fine estate in the neighborhood of Gaeta, we embarked on board a galley, which was gilded like the high altar of St. Peter's, at Rome. In our passage we were boarded by a Sallee rover. Our men defended themselves like true

Pope's soldiers; they flung themselves upon their knees, laid down their arms, and begged the corsair to give them absolution in articulo mortis.

"The Moors presently stripped us as bare as ever we were born. My mother, my maids of honor, and myself, were served all in the same manner. It is amazing how quick these gentry are at undressing people.But what surprised me most was, that they made a rude sort of surgical examination of parts of the body which are sacred to the functions of nature. I thought it a very strange kind of ceremony; for thus we are generally apt to judge of things when we have not seen the world. I afterwards learned that it was to discover if we had any diamonds concealed. This practice had been established since time immemorial among those civilized nations that scour the seas. I was informed that the religious Knights of Malta never fail to make this search whenever any Moors of either sex fall into their hands. It is a part of the law of nations, from which they never deviate.

"I need not tell you how great a hardship it was for a young princess and her mother to be made slaves and carried to Morocco.You may easily imagine what we must have suffered on board a corsair. My mother was still extremely handsome, our maids of honor, and even our common waiting–women, had more charms than were to be found in all Africa.

"As to myself, I was enchanting; I was beauty itself, and then I had my virginity. But, alas! I did not retain it long; this precious flower, which had been reserved for the lovely Prince of Massa Carrara, was cropped by the captain of the Moorish vessel, who was a hideous Negro, and thought he did me infinite honor. Indeed, both the Princess of Palestrina and myself must have had very strong constitutions to undergo all the hardships and violences we suffered before our arrival at Morocco. But I will not detain you any longer with such common things; they are hardly worth mentioning.

"Upon our arrival at Morocco we found that kingdom deluged with blood. Fifty sons of the Emperor Muley Ishmael were each at the head of a party. This produced fifty civil wars of blacks against blacks, of tawnies against tawnies, and of mulattoes against mulattoes. In short, the whole empire was one continued scene of carnage.

"No sooner were we landed than a party of blacks, of a contrary faction to that of my captain, came to rob him of his booty. Next to the money and jewels, we were the most valuable things he had. I witnessed on this occasion such a battle as you never beheld in your cold European climates. The northern nations have not that fermentation in their blood, nor that raging lust for women that is so common in Africa. The natives of Europe seem to have their veins filled with milk only; but fire and vitriol circulate in those of the inhabitants of Mount Atlas and the neighboring provinces. They fought with the fury of the lions, tigers, and serpents of their country, to decide who should have us. A Moor seized my mother by the right arm, while my captain's lieutenant held her by the left; another Moor laid hold of her by the right leg, and one of our corsairs held her by the other. In this manner almost all of our women were dragged by four soldiers.

"My captain kept me concealed behind him, and with his drawn scimitar cut down everyone who opposed him; at length I saw all our Italian women and my mother mangled and torn in pieces by the monsters who contended for them. The captives, my companions, the Moors who took us, the soldiers, the sailors, the blacks, the whites, the mulattoes, and lastly, my captain himself, were all slain, and I remained alone expiring upon a heap of dead bodies. Similar barbarous scenes were transacted every day over the whole country, which is of three hundred leagues in extent, and yet they never missed the five stated times of prayer enjoined by their prophet Mahomet.

"I disengaged myself with great difficulty from such a heap of corpses, and made a shift to crawl to a large orange tree that stood on the bank of a neighboring rivulet, where I fell down exhausted with fatigue, and overwhelmed with horror, despair, and hunger. My senses being overpowered, I fell asleep, or rather seemed to be in a trance. Thus I lay in a state of weakness and insensibility between life and death, when I felt myself pressed by something that moved up and down upon my body. This brought me to myself. I opened my eyes, and saw a pretty fair–faced man, who sighed and muttered these words between his teeth, 'O che sciagura d'essere senza coglioni!'"

CHAPTER 12

The Adventures of the Old Woman Continued

Astonished and delighted to hear my native language, and no less surprised at the young man's words, I told him that there were far greater misfortunes in the world than what he complained of. And to convince him of it, I gave him a short history of the horrible disasters that had befallen me; and as soon as I had finished, fell into a swoon again.

"He carried me in his arms to a neighboring cottage, where he had me put to bed, procured me something to eat, waited on me with the greatest attention, comforted me, caressed me, told me that he had never seen anything so perfectly beautiful as myself, and that he had never so much regretted the loss of what no one could restore to him.

"'I was born at Naples,' said he, 'where they make eunuchs of thousands of children every year; some die of the operation; some acquire voices far beyond the most tuneful of your ladies; and others are sent to govern states and empires. I underwent this operation very successfully, and was one of the singers in the Princess of Palestrina's chapel.'

"'How,' cried I, 'in my mother's chapel!'

"'The Princess of Palestrina, your mother!' cried he, bursting into a flood of tears. 'Is it possible you should be the beautiful young princess whom I had the care of bringing up till she was six years old, and who at that tender age promised to be as fair as I now behold you?'

"'I am the same,' I replied. 'My mother lies about a hundred yards from here cut in pieces and buried under a heap of dead bodies.'

"I then related to him all that had befallen me, and he in return acquainted me with all his adventures, and how he had been sent to the court of the King of Morocco by a Christian prince to conclude a treaty with that monarch; in consequence of which he was to be furnished with military stores, and ships to destroy the commerce of other Christian governments.

"'I have executed my commission,' said the eunuch; 'I am going to take ship at Ceuta, and I'll take you along with me to Italy. Ma che sciagura d'essere senza coglioni!'

"I thanked him with tears of joy, but, not withstanding, instead of taking me with him to Italy, he carried me to Algiers, and sold me to the Dey of that province. I had not been long a slave when the plague, which had made the tour of Africa, Asia, and Europe, broke out at Algiers with redoubled fury. You have seen an earthquake; but tell me, miss, have you ever had the plague?"

"Never," answered the young Baroness.

"If you had ever had it," continued the old woman, "you would own an earthquake was a trifle to it. It is very common in Africa; I was seized with it. Figure to yourself the distressed condition of the daughter of a Pope, only fifteen years old, and who in less than three months had felt the miseries of poverty and slavery; had been debauched almost every day; had beheld her mother cut into four quarters; had experienced the scourges of famine and war; and was now dying of the plague at Algiers. I did not, however, die of it; but my eunuch, and the Dey, and almost the whole seraglio of Algiers, were swept off.

"As soon as the first fury of this dreadful pestilence was over, a sale was made of the Dey's slaves. I was purchased by a merchant who carried me to Tunis. This man sold me to another merchant, who sold me again to another at Tripoli; from Tripoli I was sold to Alexandria, from Alexandria to Smyrna, and from Smyrna to Constantinople. After many changes, I at length became the property of an Aga of the Janissaries, who, soon after I came into his possession, was ordered away to the defense of Azoff, then besieged by the Russians.

"The Aga, being very fond of women, took his whole seraglio with him, and lodged us in a small fort, with two black eunuchs and twenty soldiers for our guard. Our army made a great slaughter among the Russians; but they soon returned us the compliment. Azoff was taken by storm, and the enemy spared neither age, sex, nor condition, but put all to the sword, and laid the city in ashes. Our little fort alone held out; they resolved to reduce us by famine.The twenty janissaries, who were left to defend it, had bound themselves by an oath never to surrender the place. Being reduced to the extremity of famine, they found themselves obliged to kill our two eunuchs, and eat them rather than violate their oath. But this horrible repast soon failing them, they next determined to devour the women.

"We had a very pious and humane man, who gave them a most excellent sermon on this occasion, exhorting them not to kill us all at once. 'Cut off only one of the buttocks of each of those ladies,' said he, 'and you will fare extremely well; if you are under the necessity of having recourse to the same expedient again, you will find the like supply a few days hence. Heaven will approve of so charitable an action, and work your deliverance.'

"By the force of this eloquence he easily persuaded them, and all of us underwent the operation. The man applied the same balsam as they do to children after circumcision. We were all ready to give up the ghost.

"The Janissaries had scarcely time to finish the repast with which we had supplied them, when the Russians attacked the place by means of flat–bottomed boats, and not a single janissary escaped. The Russians paid no regard to the condition we were in; but there are French surgeons in all parts of the world, and one of them took us under his care, and cured us. I shall never forget, while I live, that as soon as my wounds were perfectly healed he made me certain proposals. In general, he desired us all to be of a good cheer, assuring us that the like had happened in many sieges; and that it was perfectly agreeable to the laws of war.

"As soon as my companions were in a condition to walk, they were sent to Moscow. As for me, I fell to the lot of a Boyard, who put me to work in his garden, and gave me twenty lashes a day. But this nobleman having about two years afterwards been broken alive upon the wheel, with about thirty others, for some court intrigues, I took advantage of the event, and made my escape. I traveled over a great part of Russia. I was a long time an innkeeper's servant at Riga, then at Rostock, Wismar, Leipsic, Cassel, Utrecht, Leyden, The Hague, and Rotterdam. I have grown old in misery and disgrace, living with only one buttock, and having in perpetual remembrance that I am a Pope's daughter. I have been a hundred times upon the point of killing myself, but still I was fond of life. This ridiculous weakness is, perhaps, one of the dangerous principles implanted in our nature. For what can be more absurd than to persist in carrying a burden of which we wish to be eased? to detest, and yet to strive to preserve our existence? In a word, to caress the serpent that devours us, and hug him close to our bosoms till he has gnawed into our hearts?

"In the different countries which it has been my fate to traverse, and at the many inns where I have been a servant, I have observed a prodigious number of people who held their existence in abhorrence, and yet I never knew more than twelve who voluntarily put an end to their misery; namely, three Negroes, four Englishmen, as many Genevese, and a German professor named Robek. My last place was with the Jew, Don Issachar, who placed me near your person, my fair lady; to whose fortunes I have attached myself, and have been more concerned with your adventures than with my own. I should never have even mentioned the latter to you, had you not a little piqued me on the head of sufferings; and if it were not customary to tell stories on board a ship in order to pass away the time.

"In short, my dear miss, I have a great deal of knowledge and experience in the world, therefore take my advice: divert yourself, and prevail upon each passenger to tell his story, and if there is one of them all that has not cursed his existence many times, and said to himself over and over again that he was the most wretched of mortals, I give you leave to throw me headfirst into the sea."

CHAPTER 13

How Candide Was Obliged to Leave the Fair Cunegund and the Old Woman

The fair Cunegund, being thus made acquainted with the history of the old woman's life and adventures, paid her all the respect and civility due to a person of her rank and merit. She very readily acceded to her proposal of engaging the passengers to relate their adventures in their turns, and was at length, as well as Candide, compelled to acknowledge that the old woman was in the right.

"It is a thousand pities," said Candide, "that the sage Pangloss should have been hanged contrary to the custom of an auto–da–fe, for he would have given us a most admirable lecture on the moral and physical evil which overspreads the earth and sea; and I think I should have courage enough to presume to offer (with all due respect) some few objections."

While everyone was reciting his adventures, the ship continued on her way, and at length arrived at Buenos Ayres, where Cunegund, Captain Candide, and the old woman, landed and went to wait upon the governor, Don Fernando d'Ibaraa y Figueora y Mascarenes y Lampourdos y Souza. This nobleman carried himself with a haughtiness suitable to a person who bore so many names. He spoke with the most noble disdain to everyone, carried his nose so high, strained his voice to such a pitch, assumed so imperious an air, and stalked with so much loftiness and pride, that everyone who had the honor of conversing with him was violently tempted to bastinade His Excellency. He was immoderately fond of women, and Miss Cunegund appeared in his eyes a paragon of beauty. The first thing he did was to ask her if she was not the captain's wife. The air with which he made this demand alarmed Candide, who did not dare to say he was married to her, because indeed he was not; neither did he venture to say she was his sister, because she was not; and though a lie of this nature proved of great service to one of the ancients, and might possibly be useful to some of the moderns, yet the purity of his heart would not permit him to violate the truth.

"Miss Cunegund," replied he, "is to do me the honor to marry me, and we humbly beseech Your Excellency to condescend to grace the ceremony with your presence."

Don Fernando d'Ibaraa y Figueora y Mascarenes y Lampourdos y Souza, twirling his mustachio, and putting on a sarcastic smile, ordered Captain Candide to go and review his company. The gentle Candide obeyed, and the Governor was left with Miss Cunegund. He made her a strong declaration of love, protesting that he was ready to give her his hand in the face of the Church, or otherwise, as should appear most agreeable to a young lady of her prodigious beauty.Cunegund desired leave to retire a quarter of an hour to consult the old woman, and determine how she should proceed.

The old woman gave her the following counsel:

"Miss, you have seventy–two quarterings in your arms, it is true, but you have not a penny to bless yourself with. It is your own fault if you do not become the wife of one of the greatest noblemen in South America, with an exceeding fine mustachio. What business have you to pride yourself upon an unshaken constancy? You have been outraged by a Bulgarian soldier; a Jew and an Inquisitor have both tasted of your favors. People take advantage of misfortunes. I must confess, were I in your place, I should, without the least scruple, give my hand to the Governor, and thereby make the fortune of the brave Captain Candide."

While the old woman was thus haranguing, with all the prudence that old age and experience furnish, a small bark entered the harbor, in which was an alcayde and his alguazils. Matters had fallen out as follows.

The old woman rightly guessed that the Franciscan with the long sleeves, was the person who had taken Miss Cunegund's money and jewels, while they and Candide were at Badajoz, in their flight from Lisbon. This same friar attempted to sell some of the diamonds to a jeweler, who presently knew them to have belonged to the Grand Inquisitor, and stopped them. The Franciscan, before he was hanged, acknowledged that he had stolen them and described the persons, and the road they had taken. The flight of Cunegund and Candide was already the towntalk. They sent in pursuit of them to Cadiz; and the vessel which had been sent to make the greater dispatch, had now reached the port of Buenos Ayres. A report was spread that an alcayde was going to land, and that he was in pursuit of the murderers of My Lord, the Inquisitor. The sage old woman immediately saw what was to be done.

"You cannot run away," said she to Cunegund, "but you have nothing to fear; it was not you who killed My Lord Inquisitor: besides, as the Governor is in love with you, he will not suffer you to be ill–treated; therefore stand your ground."

Then hurrying away to Candide, she said, "Be gone hence this instant, or you will be burned alive."

Candide found there was no time to be lost; but how could he part from Cunegund, and whither must he fly for shelter?

CHAPTER 14

The Reception Candide and Cacambo Met with among the Jesuits in Paraguay

Candide had brought with him from Cadiz such a footman as one often meets with on the coasts of Spain and in the colonies. He was the fourth part of a Spaniard, of a mongrel breed, and born in Tucuman. He had successively gone through the profession of a singing boy, sexton, sailor, monk, peddler, soldier, and lackey. His name was Cacambo; he had a great affection for his master, because his master was a very good man. He immediately saddled the two Andalusian horses.

"Come, my good master, let us follow the old woman's advice, and make all the haste we can from this place without staying to look behind us."

Candide burst into a flood of tears, "O my dear Cunegund, must I then be compelled to quit you just as the Governor was going to honor us with his presence at our wedding! Cunegund, so long lost and found again, what will now become of you?"

"Lord!" said Cacambo, 'she must do as well as she can; women are never at a loss. God takes care of them, and so let us make the best of our way."

"But whither wilt thou carry me? where can we go? what can we do without Cunegund?" cried the disconsolate Candide.

"By St. James of Compostella," said Cacambo, "you were going to fight against the Jesuits of Paraguay; now let us go and fight for them; I know the road perfectly well; I'll conduct you to their kingdom; they will be delighted with a captain that understands the Bulgarian drill; you will certainly make a prodigious fortune. If we cannot succeed in this world we may in another. It is a great pleasure to see new objects and perform new exploits."

"Then you have been in Paraguay?" asked Candide.

"Ay, marry, I have," replied Cacambo. "I was a scout in the College of the Assumption, and am as well acquainted with the new government of the Los Padres as I am with the streets of Cadiz. Oh, it is an admirable government, that is most certain! The kingdom is at present upwards of three hundred leagues in diameter, and divided into thirty provinces; the fathers there are masters of everything, and the people have no money at all; this you must allow is the masterpiece of justice and reason. For my part, I see nothing so divine as the good fathers, who wage war in this part of the world against the troops of Spain and Portugal, at the same time that they hear the confessions of those very princes in Europe; who kill Spaniards in America and send them to Heaven at Madrid. This pleases me exceedingly, but let us push forward; you are going to see the happiest and most fortunate of all mortals. How charmed will those fathers be to hear that a captain who understands the Bulgarian military drill is coming to them."

As soon as they reached the first barrier, Cacambo called to the advance guard, and told them that a captain wanted to speak to My Lord, the General. Notice was given to the main guard, and immediately a Paraguayan officer ran to throw himself at the feet of the Commandant to impart this news to him. Candide and Cacambo were immediately disarmed, and their two Andalusian horses were seized. The two strangers were conducted between two files of musketeers, the Commandant was at the further end with a three–cornered cap on his head, his gown tucked up, a sword by his side, and a half–pike in his hand; he made a sign, and instantly four and twenty soldiers drew up round the newcomers. A sergeant told them that they must wait, the Commandant could not speak to them; and that the Reverend Father Provincial did not suffer any Spaniard to open his mouth but in his presence, or to stay above three hours in the province.

"And where is the Reverend Father Provincial?" said Cacambo.

"He has just come from Mass and is at the parade," replied the sergeant, "and in about three hours' time you may possibly have the honor to kiss his spurs."

"But," said Cacambo, "the Captain, who, as well as myself, is perishing of hunger, is no Spaniard, but a German; therefore, pray, might we not be permitted to break our fast till we can be introduced to His Reverence?"

The sergeant immediately went and acquainted the Commandant with what he heard.

"God be praised," said the Reverend Commandant, "since he is a German I will hear what he has to say; let him be brought to my arbor."

Immediately they conducted Candide to a beautiful pavilion adomed with a colonnade of green marble, spotted with yellow, and with an intertexture of vines, which served as a kind of cage for parrots, humming birds, guinea hens, and all other curious kinds of birds. An excellent breakfast was provided in vessels of gold; and while the Paraguayans were eating coarse Indian corn out of wooden dishes in the open air, and exposed to the burning heat of the sun, the Reverend Father Commandant retired to his cool arbor.

He was a very handsome young man, round–faced, fair, and fresh–colored, his eyebrows were finely arched, he had a piercing eye, the tips of his ears were red, his lips vermilion, and he had a bold and commanding air; but such a boldness as neither resembled that of a Spaniard nor of a Jesuit. He ordered Candide and Cacambo to have their arms restored to them, together with their two Andalusian horses.Cacambo gave the poor beasts some oats to eat close by the arbor, keeping a strict eye upon them all the while for fear of surprise.

Candide having kissed the hem of the Commandant's robe, they sat down to table.

"It seems you are a German," said the Jesuit to him in that language.

"Yes, Reverend Father," answered Candide.

As they pronounced these words they looked at each other with great amazement and with an emotion that neither could conceal.

"From what part of Germany do you come?" said the Jesuit.

"From the dirty province of Westphalia," answered Candide.

"I was born in the castle of Thunder–ten–tronckh."

"Oh heavens! is it possible?" said the Commandant.

"What a miracle!" cried Candide.

"Can it be you?" said the Commandant.

On this they both drew a few steps backwards, then running into each other's arms, embraced, and wept profusely.

"Is it you then, Reverend Father? You are the brother of the fair Miss Cunegund? You that was slain by the Bulgarians! You the Baron's son! You a Jesuit in Paraguay! I must confess this is a strange world we live in. O Pangloss! what joy would this have given you if you had not been hanged."

The Commandant dismissed the Negro slaves, and the Paraguayans who presented them with liquor in crystal goblets. He returned thanks to God and St. Ignatius a thousand times; he clasped Candide in his arms, and both their faces were bathed in tears.

"You will be more surprised, more affected, more transported," said Candide, "when I tell you that Miss Cunegund, your sister, whose belly was supposed to have been ripped open, is in perfect health."

"In your neighborhood, with the Governor of Buenos Ayres; and I myself was going to fight against you."

Every word they uttered during this long conversation was productive of some new matter of astonishment. Their souls fluttered on their tongues, listened in their ears, and sparkled in their eyes. Like true Germans, they continued a long while at table, waiting for the Reverend Father; and the Commandant spoke to his dear Candide as follows.

CHAPTER 15

How Candide Killed the Brother of His Dear Cunegund

Never while I live shall I lose the remembrance of that horrible day on which I saw my father and mother barbarously butchered before my eyes, and my sister ravished. When the Bulgarians retired we searched in vain for my dear sister. She was nowhere to be found; but the bodies of my father, mother, and myself, with two servant maids and three little boys, all of whom had been murdered by the remorseless enemy, were thrown into a cart to be buried in a chapel belonging to the Jesuits, within two leagues of our family seat. A Jesuit sprinkled us with some holy water, which was confounded salty, and a few drops of it went into my eyes; the father perceived that my eyelids stirred a little; he put his hand upon my breast and felt my heartbeat; upon which he gave me proper assistance, and at the end of three weeks I was perfectly recovered. You know, my dear Candide, I was very handsome; I became still more so, and the Reverend Father Croust, superior of that house, took a great fancy to me; he gave me the habit of the order, and some years afterwards I was sent to Rome. Our General stood in need of new recruits of young German Jesuits. The sovereigns of Paraguay admit of as few Spanish Jesuits as possible; they prefer those of other nations, as being more obedient to command. The Reverend Father General looked upon me as a proper person to work in that vineyard. I set out in company with a Polander and a Tyrolese. Upon my arrival I was honored with a subdeaconship and a lieutenancy. Now I am colonel and priest. We shall give a warm reception to the King of Spain's troops; I can assure you they will be well excommunicated and beaten. Providence has sent you hither to assist us. But is it true that my dear sister Cunegund is in the neighborhood with the Governor of Buenos Ayres?"

Candide swore that nothing could be more true; and the tears began again to trickle down their cheeks. The Baron knew no end of embracing Candide, be called him his brother, his deliverer.

"Perhaps," said he, "my dear Candide, we shall be fortunate enough to enter the town, sword in hand, and recover my sister Cunegund."

"Ah! that would crown my wishes," replied Candide; "for I intended to marry her; and I hope I shall still be able to effect it."

"Insolent fellow!" cried the Baron. "You! you have the impudence to marry my sister, who bears seventy–two quarterings! Really, I think you have an insufferable degree of assurance to dare so much as to mention such an audacious design to me."

Candide, thunderstruck at the oddness of this speech, answered:

"Reverend Father, all the quarterings in the world are of no signification. I have delivered your sister from a Jew and an Inquisitor; she is under many obligations to me, and she is resolved to give me her hand. My master, Pangloss, always told me that mankind are by nature equal. Therefore, you may depend upon it that I will marry your sister."

"We shall see to that, villain!" said the Jesuit, Baron of Thunder–ten–tronckh, and struck him across the face with the flat side of his sword. Candide in an instant drew his rapier and plunged it up to the hilt in the Jesuit's body; but in pulling it out reeking hot, he burst into tears.

"Good God!" cried he, "I have killed my old master, my friend, my brother–in–law. I am the best man in the world, and yet I have already killed three men, and of these three, two were priests."

Cacambo, who was standing sentry near the door of the arbor, instantly ran up.

"Nothing remains," said his master, "but to sell our lives as dearly as possible; they will undoubtedly look into the arbor; we must die sword in hand."

Cacambo, who had seen many of this kind of adventures, was not discouraged. He stripped the Baron of his Jesuit's habit and put it upon Candide, then gave him the dead man's three–cornered cap and made him mount on horseback. All this was done as quick as thought.

"Gallop, master," cried Cacambo; "everybody will take you for a Jesuit going to give orders; and we shall have passed the frontiers before they will be able to overtake us."

He flew as he spoke these words, crying out aloud in Spanish, "Make way; make way for the Reverend Father Colonel."

CHAPTER 16

What Happened to Our Two Travelers with Two Girls, Two Monkeys, and the Savages, Called Oreillons

Candide and his valet had already passed the frontiers before it was known that the German Jesuit was dead. The wary Cacambo had taken care to fill his wallet with bread, chocolate, some ham, some fruit, and a few bottles of wine. They penetrated with their Andalusian horses into a strange country, where they could discover no beaten path. At length a beautiful meadow, intersected with purling rills, opened to their view. Cacambo proposed to his master to take some nourishment, and he set him an example.

"How can you desire me to feast upon ham, when I have killed the Baron's son and am doomed never more to see the beautiful Cunegund?What will it avail me to prolong a wretched life that must be spent far from her in remorse and despair? And then what will the journal of Trevoux say?" was Candide's reply.

While he was making these reflections he still continued eating. The sun was now on the point of setting when the ears of our two wanderers were assailed with cries which seemed to be uttered by a female voice.They could not tell whether these were cries of grief or of joy; however, they instantly started up, full of that inquietude and apprehension which a strange place naturally inspires. The cries proceeded from two young women who were tripping disrobed along the mead, while two monkeys followed close at their heels biting at their limbs. Candide was touched with compassion; he had learned to shoot while he was among the Bulgarians, and he could hit a filbert in a hedge without touching a leaf. Accordingly he took up his double–barrelled Spanish gun, pulled the trigger, and laid the two monkeys lifeless on the ground.

"God be praised, my dear Cacambo, I have rescued two poor girls from a most perilous situation; if I have committed a sin in killing an Inquisitor and a Jesuit, I have made ample amends by saving the lives of these two distressed damsels. Who knows but they may be young ladies of a good family, and that the assistance I have been so happy to give them may procure us great advantage in this country?"

He was about to continue when he felt himself struck speechless at seeing the two girls embracing the dead bodies of the monkeys in the tenderest manner, bathing their wounds with their tears, and rending the air with the most doleful lamentations.

"Really," said he to Cacambo, "I should not have expected to see such a prodigious share of good nature."

"Master," replied the knowing valet, "you have made a precious piece of work of it; do you know that you have killed the lovers of these two ladies?"

"Their lovers! Cacambo, you are jesting! It cannot be! I can never believe it."

"Dear sir," replied Cacambo, "you are surprised at everything. Why should you think it so strange that there should be a country where monkeys insinuate themselves into the good graces of the ladies?They are the fourth part of a man as I am the fourth part of a Spaniard."

"Alas!" replied Candide, "I remember to have heard my master Pangloss say that such accidents as these frequently came to pass in former times, and that these commixtures are productive of centaurs, fauns, and satyrs; and that many of the ancients had seen such monsters; but I looked upon the whole as fabulous."

"Now you are convinced," said Cacambo, "that it is very true, and you see what use is made of those creatures by persons who have not had a proper education; all I am afraid of is that these same ladies may play us some ugly trick."

These judicious reflections operated so far on Candide as to make him quit the meadow and strike into a thicket. There he and Cacambo supped, and after heartily cursing the Grand Inquisitor, the Governor of Buenos Ayres, and the Baron, they fell asleep on the ground. When they awoke they were surprised to find that they could not move; the reason was that the Oreillons who inhabit that country, and to whom the ladies had given information of these two strangers, had bound them with cords made of the bark of trees. They saw themselves surrounded by fifty naked Oreillons armed with bows and arrows, clubs, and hatchets of flint; some were making a fire under a large cauldron; and others were preparing spits, crying out one and all, "A Jesuit! a Jesuit! we shall be revenged; we shall have excellent cheer; let us eat this Jesuit; let us eat him up."

"I told you, master," cried Cacambo, mournfully, "that these two wenches would play us some scurvy trick."

Candide, seeing the cauldron and the spits, cried out, "I suppose they are going either to boil or roast us. Ah! what would Pangloss say if he were to see how pure nature is formed? Everything is right; it may be so; but I must confess it is something hard to be bereft of dear Miss Cunegund, and to be spitted like a rabbit by these barbarous Oreillons."

Cacambo, who never lost his presence of mind in distress, said to the disconsolate Candide, "Do not despair; I understand a little of the jargon of these people; I will speak to them."

"Ay, pray do," said Candide, "and be sure you make them sensible of the horrid barbarity of boiling and roasting human creatures, and how little of Christianity there is in such practices."

"Gentlemen," said Cacambo, "you think perhaps you are going to feast upon a Jesuit; if so, it is mighty well; nothing can be more agreeable to justice than thus to treat your enemies. Indeed the law of nature teaches us to kill our neighbor, and accordingly we find this practiced all over the world; and if we do not indulge ourselves in eating human flesh, it is because we have much better fare; but for your parts, who have not such resources as we, it is certainly much better judged to feast upon your enemies than to throw their bodies to the fowls of the air; and thus lose all the fruits of your victory.

"But surely, gentlemen, you would not choose to eat your friends. You imagine you are going to roast a Jesuit, whereas my master is your friend, your defender, and you are going to spit the very man who has been destroying your enemies; as to myself, I am your countryman; this gentleman is my master, and so far from being a Jesuit, give me leave to tell you he has very lately killed one of that order, whose spoils he now wears, and which have probably occasioned your mistake. To convince you of the truth of what I say, take the habit he has on and carry it to the first barrier of the Jesuits' kingdom, and inquire whether my master did not kill one of their officers. There will be little or no time lost by this, and you may still reserve our bodies in your power to feast on if you should find what we have told you to be false. But, on the contrary, if you find it to be true, I am persuaded you are too well acquainted with the principles of the laws of society, humanity, and justice, not to use us courteously, and suffer us to depart unhurt."

This speech appeared very reasonable to the Oreillons; they deputed two of their people with all expedition to inquire into the truth of this affair, who acquitted themselves of their commission like men of sense, and soon returned with good tidings for our distressed adventurers. Upon this they were loosed, and those who were so lately going to roast and boil them now showed them all sorts of civilities, offered them girls, gave them refreshments, and reconducted them to the confines of their country, crying before them all the way, in token of joy, "He is no Jesuit! he is no Jesuit!"

Candide could not help admiring the cause of his deliverance."What men! what manners!" cried he. "If I had not fortunately run my sword up to the hilt in the body of Miss Cunegund's brother, I should have certainly been eaten alive. But, after all, pure nature is an excellent thing; since these people, instead of eating me, showed me a thousand civilities as soon as they knew was not a Jesuit."

CHAPTER 17

Candide and His Valet Arrive in the Country of El Dorado – What They Saw There

When to the frontiers of the Oreillons, said Cacambo to Candide, "You see, this hemisphere is not better than the other; now take my advice and let us return to Europe by the shortest way possible."

"But how can we get back?" said Candide; "and whither shall we go?To my own country? The Bulgarians and the Abares are laying that waste with fire and sword. Or shall we go to Portugal? There I shall be burned; and if we abide here we are every moment in danger of being spitted. But how can I bring myself to quit that part of the world where my dear Miss Cunegund has her residence?"

"Let us return towards Cayenne," said Cacambo. "There we shall meet with some Frenchmen, for you know those gentry ramble all over the world. Perhaps they will assist us, and God will look with pity on our distress."

It was not so easy to get to Cayenne. They knew pretty nearly whereabouts it lay; but the mountains, rivers, precipices, robbers, savages, were dreadful obstacles in the way. Their horses died with fatigue and their provisions were at an end. They subsisted a whole month on wild fruit, till at length they came to a little river bordered with cocoa trees; the sight of which at once revived their drooping spirits and furnished nourishment for their enfeebled bodies.

Cacambo, who was always giving as good advice as the old woman herself, said to Candide, "You see there is no holding out any longer; we have traveled enough on foot. I spy an empty canoe near the river side; let us fill it with cocoanuts, get into it, and go down with the stream; a river always leads to some inhabited place. If we do not meet with agreeable things, we shall at least meet with something new."

"Agreed," replied Candide; "let us recommend ourselves to Providence."

They rowed a few leagues down the river, the banks of which were in some places covered with flowers; in others barren; in some parts smooth and level, and in others steep and rugged. The stream widened as they went further on, till at length it passed under one of the frightful rocks, whose summits seemed to reach the clouds. Here our two travelers had the courage to commit themselves to the stream, which, contracting in this part, hurried them along with a dreadful noise and rapidity.

At the end of four and twenty hours they saw daylight again; but their canoe was dashed to pieces against the rocks. They were obliged to creep along, from rock to rock, for the space of a league, till at length a spacious plain presented itself to their sight. This place was bounded by a chain of inaccessible mountains.The country appeared cultivated equally for pleasure and to produce the necessaries of life. The useful and agreeable were here equally blended. The roads were covered, or rather adorned, with carriages formed of glittering materials, in which were men and women of a surprising beauty, drawn with great rapidity by red sheep of a very large size; which far surpassed the finest coursers of Andalusian Tetuan, or Mecquinez.

"Here is a country, however," said Candide, "preferable to Westphalia."

He and Cacambo landed near the first village they saw, at the entrance of which they perceived some children covered with tattered garments of the richest brocade, playing at quoits. Our two inhabitants of the other hemisphere amused themselves greatly with what they saw. The quoits were large, round pieces, yellow, red, and green, which cast a most glorious luster. Our travelers picked some of them up, and they proved to be gold, emeralds, rubies, and diamonds; the least of which would have been the greatest ornament to the superb throne of the Great Mogul.

"Without doubt," said Cacambo, "those children must be the King's sons that are playing at quoits."

As he was uttering these words the schoolmaster of the village appeared, who came to call the children to school.

"There," said Candide, "is the preceptor of the royal family."

The little ragamuffins immediately quitted their diversion, leaving the quoits on the ground with all their other playthings.Candide gathered them up, ran to the schoolmaster, and, with a most respectful bow, presented them to him, giving him to understand by signs that their Royal Highnesses had forgot their gold and precious stones. The schoolmaster, with a smile, flung them upon the ground, then examining Candide from head to foot with an air of admiration, he turned his back and went on his way.

Our travelers took care, however, to gather up the gold, the rubies, and the emeralds.

"Where are we?" cried Candide. "The King's children in this country must have an excellent education, since they are taught to show such a contempt for gold and precious stones."

Cacambo was as much surprised as his master. They then drew near the first house in the village, which was built after the manner of a European palace. There was a crowd of people about the door, and a still greater number in the house. The sound of the most delightful instruments of music was heard, and the most agreeable smell came from the kitchen. Cacambo went up to the door and heard those within talking in the Peruvian language, which was his mother tongue; for everyone knows that Cacambo was born in a village of Tucuman, where no other language is spoken.

"I will be your interpreter here," said he to Candide. "Let us go in; this is an eating house."

Immediately two waiters and two servant–girls, dressed in cloth of gold, and their hair braided with ribbons of tissue, accosted the strangers and invited them to sit down to the ordinary. Their dinner consisted of four dishes of different soups, each garnished with two young paroquets, a large dish of bouille that weighed two hundred weight, two roasted monkeys of a delicious flavor, three hundred hummingbirds in one dish, and six hundred flybirds in another; some excellent ragouts, delicate tarts, and the whole served up in dishes of rock–crystal. Several sorts of liquors, extracted from the sugarcane, were handed about by the servants who attended.

Most of the company were chapmen and wagoners, all extremely polite; they asked Cacambo a few questions with the utmost discretion and circumspection; and replied to his in a most obliging and satisfactory manner.

As soon as dinner was over, both Candide and Cacambo thought they should pay very handsomely for their entertainment by laying down two of those large gold pieces which they had picked off the ground; but the landlord and landlady burst into a fit of laughing and held their sides for some time.

When the fit was over, the landlord said, "Gentlemen, I plainly perceive you are strangers, and such we are not accustomed to charge; pardon us, therefore, for laughing when you offered us the common pebbles of our highways for payment of your reckoning. To be sure, you have none of the coin of this kingdom; but there is no necessity of having any money at all to dine in this house. All the inns, which are established for the convenience of those who carry on the trade of this nation, are maintained by the government. You have found but very indifferent entertainment here, because this is only a poor village; but in almost every other of these public houses you will meet with a reception worthy of persons of your merit."

Cacambo explained the whole of this speech of the landlord to Candide, who listened to it with the same astonishment with which his friend communicated it.

"What sort of a country is this," said the one to the other, "that is unknown to all the world; and in which Nature has everywhere so different an appearance to what she has in ours? Possibly this is that part of the globe where everywhere is right, for there must certainly be some such place. And, for all that Master Pangloss could say, I often perceived that things went very ill in Westphalia."

CHAPTER 18

What They Saw in the Country of El Dorado

Cacambo vented all his curiosity upon his landlord by a thousand different questions; the honest man answered him thus, "I am very ignorant, sir, but I am contented with my ignorance; however, we have in this neighborhood an old man retired from court, who is the most learned and communicative person in the whole kingdom."

He then conducted Cacambo to the old man; Candide acted now only a second character, and attended his valet. They entered a very plain house, for the door was nothing but silver, and the ceiling was only of beaten gold, but wrought in such elegant taste as to vie with the richest. The antechamber, indeed, was only incrusted with rubies and emeralds; but the order in which everything was disposed made amends for this great simplicity.

The old man received the strangers on his sofa, which was stuffed with hummingbirds' feathers; and ordered his servants to present them with liquors in golden goblets, after which he satisfied their curiosity in the following terms.

"I am now one hundred and seventy–two years old, and I learned of my late father, who was equerry to the King, the amazing revolutions of Peru, to which he had been an eyewitness. This kingdom is the ancient patrimony of the Incas, who very imprudently quitted it to conquer another part of the world, and were at length conquered and destroyed themselves by the Spaniards.

"Those princes of their family who remained in their native country acted more wisely. They ordained, with the consent of their whole nation, that none of the inhabitants of our little kingdom should ever quit it; and to this wise ordinance we owe the preservation of our innocence and happiness. The Spaniards had some confused notion of this country, to which they gave the name of El Dorado; and Sir Walter Raleigh, an Englishman, actually came very near it about three hundred years ago; but the inaccessible rocks and precipices with which our country is surrounded on all sides, has hitherto secured us from the rapacious fury of the people of Europe, who have an unaccountable fondness for the pebbles and dirt of our land, for the sake of which they would murder us all to the very last man."

The conversation lasted some time and turned chiefly on the form of government, their manners, their women, their public diversions, and the arts. At length, Candide, who had always had a taste for metaphysics, asked whether the people of that country had any religion.

The old man reddened a little at this question.

"Can you doubt it?" said he; "do you take us for wretches lost to all sense of gratitude?"

Cacambo asked in a respectful manner what was the established religion of El Dorado. The old man blushed again and said, "Can there be two religions, then? Ours, I apprehend, is the religion of the whole world; we worship God from morning till night."

"Do you worship but one God?" said Cacambo, who still acted as the interpreter of Candide's doubts.

"Certainly," said the old man; "there are not two, nor three, nor four Gods. I must confess the people of your world ask very extraordinary questions."

However, Candide could not refrain from making many more inquiries of the old man; he wanted to know in what manner they prayed to God in El Dorado.

"We do not pray to Him at all," said the reverend sage; "we have nothing to ask of Him, He has given us all we want, and we give Him thanks incessantly."

Candide had a curiosity to see some of their priests, and desired Cacambo to ask the old man where they were. At which he smiling said, "My friends, we are all of us priests; the King and all the heads of families sing solemn hymns of thanksgiving every morning, accompanied by five or six thousand musicians."

"What!" said Cacambo, "have you no monks among you to dispute, to govern, to intrigue, and to burn people who are not of the same opinion with themselves?"

"Do you take us for fools?" said the old man. "Here we are all of one opinion, and know not what you mean by your monks."

During the whole of this discourse Candide was in raptures, and he said to himself, "What a prodigious difference is there between this place and Westphalia; and this house and the Baron's castle. Ah, Master Pangloss! had you ever seen El Dorado, you would no longer have maintained that the castle of Thunder–ten–tronckh was the finest of all possible edifices; there is nothing like seeing the world, that's certain."

This long conversation being ended, the old man ordered six sheep to be harnessed and put to the coach, and sent twelve of his servants to escort the travelers to court.

"Excuse me," said he, "for not waiting on you in person, my age deprives me of that honor. The King will receive you in such a manner that you will have no reason to complain; and doubtless you will make a proper allowance for the customs of the country if they should not happen altogether to please you."

Candide and Cacambo got into the coach, the six sheep flew, and, in less than a quarter of an hour, they arrived at the King's palace, which was situated at the further end of the capital. At the entrance was a portal two hundred and twenty feet high and one hundred wide; but it is impossible for words to express the materials of which it was built. The reader, however, will readily conceive that they must have a prodigious superiority over the pebbles and sand, which we call gold and precious stones.

Twenty beautiful young virgins in waiting received Candide and Cacambo on their alighting from the coach, conducted them to the bath and clad them in robes woven of the down of hummingbirds; after which they were introduced by the great officers of the crown of both sexes to the King's apartment, between two files of musicians, each file consisting of a thousand, agreeable to the custom of the country.

When they drew near to the presence–chamber, Cacambo asked one of the officers in what manner they were to pay their obeisance to His Majesty; whether it was the custom to fall upon their knees, or to prostrate themselves upon the ground; whether they were to put their hands upon their heads, or behind their backs; whether they were to lick the dust off the floor; in short, what was the ceremony usual on such occasions.

"The custom," said the great officer, "is to embrace the King and kiss him on each cheek."

Candide and Cacambo accordingly threw their arms round His Majesty's neck, who received them in the most gracious manner imaginable, and very politely asked them to sup with him.

While supper was preparing, orders were given to show them the city, where they saw public structures that reared their lofty heads to the clouds; the marketplaces decorated with a thousand columns; fountains of spring water, besides others of rose water, and of liquors drawn from the sugarcane, incessantly flowing in the great squares, which were paved with a kind of precious stones that emitted an odor like that of cloves and cinnamon.

Candide asked to see the High Court of justice, the Parliament; but was answered that they had none in that country, being utter strangers to lawsuits. He then inquired if they had any prisons; they replied none. But what gave him at once the greatest surprise and pleasure was the Palace of Sciences, where he saw a gallery two thousand feet long, filled with the various apparatus in mathematics and natural philosophy.

After having spent the whole afternoon in seeing only about the thousandth part of the city, they were brought back to the King's palace. Candide sat down at the table with His Majesty, his valet Cacambo, and several ladies of the court. Never was entertainment more elegant, nor could any one possibly show more wit than His Majesty displayed while they were at supper. Cacambo explained all the King's bons mots to Candide, and, although they were translated, they still appeared to be bons mots. Of all the things that surprised Candide, this was not the least.

They spent a whole month in this hospitable place, during which time Candide was continually saying to Cacambo, "I own, my friend, once more, that the castle where I was born is a mere nothing in comparison to the place where we now are; but still Miss Cunegund is not here, and you yourself have doubtless some fair one in Europe for whom you sigh. If we remain here we shall only be as others are; whereas if we return to our own world with only a dozen of El Dorado sheep, loaded with the pebbles of this country, we shall be richer than all the kings in Europe; we shall no longer need to stand in awe of the Inquisitors; and we may easily recover Miss Cunegund."

This speech was perfectly agreeable to Cacambo. A fondness for roving, for making a figure in their own country, and for boasting of what they had seen in their travels, was so powerful in our two wanderers that they resolved to be no longer happy; and demanded permission of the King to quit the country.

"You are about to do a rash and silly action," said the King. "I am sensible my kingdom is an inconsiderable spot; but when people are tolerably at their ease in any place, I should think it would be to their interest to remain there. Most assuredly, I have no right to detain you, or any strangers, against your wills; this is an act of tyranny to which our manners and our laws are equally repugnant. All men are by nature free; you have therefore an undoubted liberty to depart whenever you please, but you will have many and great difficulties to encounter in passing the frontiers. It is impossible to ascend that rapid river which runs under high and vaulted rocks, and by which you were conveyed hither by a kind of miracle. The mountains by which my kingdom are hemmed in on all sides, are ten thousand feet high, and perfectly perpendicular; they are above ten leagues across, and the descent from them is one continued precipice.

"However, since you are determined to leave us, I will immediately give orders to the superintendent of my carriages to cause one to be made that will convey you very safely. When they have conducted you to the back of the mountains, nobody can attend you farther; for my subjects have made a vow never to quit the kingdom, and they are too prudent to break it. Ask me whatever else you please."

"All we shall ask of Your Majesty," said Cacambo, "is only a few sheep laden with provisions, pebbles, and the clay of your country."

The King smiled at the request and said, "I cannot imagine what pleasure you Europeans find in our yellow clay; but take away as much of it as you will, and much good may it do you."

He immediately gave orders to his engineers to make a machine to hoist these two extraordinary men out of the kingdom. Three thousand good machinists went to work and finished it in about fifteen days, and it did not cost more than twenty millions sterling of that country's money. Candide and Cacambo were placed on this machine, and they took with them two large red sheep, bridled and saddled, to ride upon, when they got on the other side of the mountains; twenty others to serve as sumpters for carrying provisions; thirty laden with presents of whatever was most curious in the country, and fifty with gold, diamonds, and other precious stones. The King, at parting with our two adventurers, embraced them with the greatest cordiality.

It was a curious sight to behold the manner of their setting off, and the ingenious method by which they and their sheep were hoisted to the top of the mountains. The machinists and engineers took leave of them as soon as they had conveyed them to a place of safety, and Candide was wholly occupied with the thoughts of presenting his sheep to Miss Cunegund.

"Now," cried he, "thanks to Heaven, we have more than sufficient to pay the Governor of Buenos Ayres for Miss Cunegund, if she is redeemable. Let us make the best of our way to Cayenne, where we will take shipping and then we may at leisure think of what kingdom we shall purchase with our riches."

CHAPTER 19

What Happened to Them at Surinam, and How Candide Became Acquainted with Martin

Our travelers' first day's journey was very pleasant; they were elated with the prospect of possessing more riches than were to be found in Europe, Asia, and Africa together. Candide, in amorous transports, cut the name of Miss Cunegund on almost every tree he came to. The second day two of their sheep sunk in a morass, and were swallowed up with their Jading; two more died of fatigue; some few days afterwards seven or eight perished with hunger in a desert, and others, at different times, tumbled down precipices, or were otherwise lost, so that, after traveling about a hundred days they had only two sheep left of the hundred and two they brought with them from El Dorado.

Said Candide to Cacambo, "You see, my dear friend, how perishable the riches of this world are; there is nothing solid but virtue."

"Very true," said Cacambo, "but we have still two sheep remaining, with more treasure than ever the King of Spain will be possessed of; and I espy a town at a distance, which I take to be Surinam, a town belonging to the Dutch. We are now at the end of our troubles, and at the beginning of happiness."

As they drew near the town they saw a Negro stretched on the ground with only one half of his habit, which was a kind of linen frock; for the poor man had lost his left leg and his right hand.

"Good God," said Candide in Dutch, "what dost thou here, friend, in this deplorable condition?"

"I am waiting for my master, Mynheer Vanderdendur, the famous trader," answered the Negro.

"Was it Mynheer Vanderdendur that used you in this cruel manner?"

"Yes, sir," said the Negro; "it is the custom here. They give a linen garment twice a year, and that is all our covering. When we labor in the sugar works, and the mill happens to snatch hold of a finger, they instantly chop off our hand; and when we attempt to run away, they cut off a leg. Both these cases have happened to me, and it is at this expense that you eat sugar in Europe; and yet when my mother sold me for ten patacoons on the coast of Guinea, she said to me, 'My dear child, bless our fetishes; adore them forever; they will make thee live happy; thou hast the honor to be a slave to our lords the whites, by which thou wilt make the fortune of us thy parents.'

"Alas! I know not whether I have made their fortunes; but they have not made mine; dogs, monkeys, and parrots are a thousand times less wretched than I. The Dutch fetishes who converted me tell me every Sunday that the blacks and whites are all children of one father, whom they call Adam. As for me, I do not understand anything of genealogies; but if what these preachers say is true, we are all second cousins; and you must allow that it is impossible to be worse treated by our relations than we are."

"O Pangloss!" cried out Candide, "such horrid doings never entered thy imagination. Here is an end of the matter. I find myself, after all, obliged to renounce thy Optimism."

"Optimism," said Cacambo, "what is that?"

"Alas!" replied Candide, "it is the obstinacy of maintaining that everything is best when it is worst."

And so saying he turned his eyes towards the poor Negro, and shed a flood of tears; and in this weeping mood he entered the town of Surinam.

Immediately upon their arrival our travelers inquired if there was any vessel in the harbor which they might send to Buenos Ayres. The person they addressed themselves to happened to be the master of a Spanish bark, who offered to agree with them on moderate terms, and appointed them a meeting at a public house. Thither Candide and his faithful Cacambo went to wait for him, taking with them their two sheep.

Candide, who was all frankness and sincerity, made an ingenuous recital of his adventures to the Spaniard, declaring to him at the same time his resolution of carrying off Miss Cunegund from the Governor of Buenos Ayres.

"Oh, ho!" said the shipmaster, "if that is the case, get whom you please to carry you to Buenos Ayres; for my part, I wash my hands of the affair. It would prove a hanging matter to us all. The fair Cunegund is the Governor's favorite mistress."

These words were like a clap of thunder to Candide; he wept bitterly for a long time, and, taking Cacambo aside, he said to him, "I'll tell you, my dear friend, what you must do. We have each of us in our pockets to the value of five or six millions in diamonds; you are cleverer at these matters than I; you must go to Buenos Ayres and bring off Miss Cunegund. If the Governor makes any difficulty give him a million; if he holds out, give him two; as you have not killed an

Inquisitor, they will have no suspicion of you. I'll fit out another ship and go to Venice, where I will wait for you. Venice is a free country, where we shall have nothing to fear from Bulgarians, Abares, Jews or Inquisitors."

Cacambo greatly applauded this wise resolution. He was inconsolable at the thoughts of parting with so good a master, who treated him more like an intimate friend than a servant; but the pleasure of being able to do him a service soon got the better of his sorrow. They embraced each other with a flood of tears. Candide charged him not to forget the old woman. Cacambo set out the same day.This Cacambo was a very honest fellow.

Candide continued some days longer at Surinam, waiting for any captain to carry him and his two remaining sheep to Italy. He hired domestics, and purchased many things necessary for a long voyage; at length Mynheer Vanderdendur, skipper of a large Dutch vessel, came and offered his service.

"What will you have," said Candide, "to carry me, my servants, my baggage, and these two sheep you see here, directly to Venice?"

The skipper asked ten thousand piastres, and Candide agreed to his demand without hestitation.

"Ho, ho!" said the cunning Vanderdendur to himself, "this stranger must be very rich; he agrees to give me ten thousand piastres without hesitation."

Returning a little while after, he told Candide that upon second consideration he could not undertake the voyage for less than twenty thousand.

"Very well; you shall have them," said Candide.

"Zounds!" said the skipper to himself, "this man agrees to pay twenty thousand piastres with as much ease as ten."

Accordingly he went back again, and told him roundly that he would not carry him to Venice for less than thirty thousand piastres.

"Then you shall have thirty thousand," said Candide.

"Odso!" said the Dutchman once more to himself, "thirty thousand piastres seem a trifle to this man. Those sheep must certainly be laden with an immense treasure. I'll e'en stop here and ask no more; but make him pay down the thirty thousand piastres, and then we may see what is to be done farther."

Candide sold two small diamonds, the least of which was worth more than all the skipper asked. He paid him beforehand, the two sheep were put on board, and Candide followed in a small boat to join the vessel in the road. The skipper took advantage of his opportunity, hoisted sail, and put out to sea with a favorable wind. Candide, confounded and amazed, soon lost sight of the ship.

"Alas!" said he, "this is a trick like those in our old world!"

He returned back to the shore overwhelmed with grief; and, indeed, he had lost what would have made the fortune of twenty monarchs.

Straightway upon his landing he applied to the Dutch magistrate; being transported with passion he thundered at the door, which being opened, he went in, told his case, and talked a little louder than was necessary. The magistrate began with fining him ten thousand piastres for his petulance, and then listened very patiently to what he had to say, promised to examine into the affair on the skipper's return, and ordered him to pay ten thousand piastres more for the fees of the court.

This treatment put Candide out of all patience; it is true, he had suffered misfortunes a thousand times more grievous, but the cool insolence of the judge, and the villainy of the skipper raised his choler and threw him into a deep melancholy. The villainy of mankind presented itself to his mind in all its deformity, and his soul was a prey to the most gloomy ideas. After some time, hearing that the captain of a French ship was ready to set sail for Bordeaux, as he had no more sheep loaded with diamonds to put on board, he hired the cabin at the usual price; and made it known in the town that he would pay the passage and board of any honest man who would give him his company during the voyage; besides making him a present of ten thousand piastres, on condition that such person was the most dissatisfied with his condition, and the most unfortunate in the whole province.

Upon this there appeared such a crowd of candidates that a large fleet could not have contained them. Candide, willing to choose from among those who appeared most likely to answer his intention, selected twenty, who seemed to him the most sociable, and who all pretended to merit the preference. He invited them to his inn, and promised to treat them with a supper, on condition that every man should bind himself by an oath to relate his own history; declaring at the same time, that he would make choice of that person who should appear to him the most deserving of compassion, and the most justly dissatisfied with his condition in life; and that he would make a present to the rest.

This extraordinary assembly continued sitting till four in the morning. Candide, while he was listening to their adventures, called to mind what the old woman had said to him in their voyage to Buenos Ayres, and the wager she had laid that there was not a person on board the ship but had met with great misfortunes. Every story he heard put him in mind of Pangloss.

"My old master," said he, "would be confoundedly put to it to demonstrate his favorite system. Would he were here! Certainly if everything is for the best, it is in El Dorado, and not in the other parts of the world."

At length he determined in favor of a poor scholar, who had labored ten years for the booksellers at Amsterdam: being of opinion that no employment could be more detestable.

This scholar, who was in fact a very honest man, had been robbed by his wife, beaten by his son, and forsaken by his daughter, who had run away with a Portuguese. He had been likewise deprived of a small employment on which he subsisted, and he was persecuted by the clergy of Surinam, who took him for a Socinian. It must be acknowledged that the other competitors were, at least, as wretched as he; but Candide was in hopes that the company of a man of letters would relieve the tediousness of the voyage. All the other candidates complained that Candide had done them great injustice, but he stopped their mouths by a present of a hundred piastres to each.

CHAPTER 20

What Befell Candide and Martin on Their Passage

The old philosopher, whose name was Martin, took shipping with Candide for Bordeaux. Both had seen and suffered a great deal, and had the ship been going from Surinam to Japan round the Cape of Good Hope, they could have found sufficient entertainment for each other during the whole voyage, in discoursing upon moral and natural evil.

Candide, however, had one advantage over Martin: he lived in the pleasing hopes of seeing Miss Cunegund once more; whereas, the poor philosopher had nothing to hope for. Besides, Candide had money and jewels, and, not withstanding he had lost a hundred red sheep laden with the greatest treasure outside of El Dorado, and though he still smarted from the reflection of the Dutch skipper's knavery, yet when he considered what he had still left, and repeated the name of Cunegund, especially after meal times, he inclined to Pangloss's doctrine.

"And pray," said he to Martin, "what is your opinion of the whole of this system? What notion have you of moral and natural evil?"

"Sir," replied Martin, "our priest accused me of being a Socinian; but the real truth is, I am a Manichaean."

"Nay, now you are jesting," said Candide; "there are no Manichaeans existing at present in the world."

"And yet I am one," said Martin; "but I cannot help it. I cannot for the soul of me think otherwise."

"Surely the Devil must be in you," said Candide.

"He concerns himself so much," replied Martin, "in the affairs of this world that it is very probable he may be in me as well as everywhere else; but I must confess, when I cast my eye on this globe, or rather globule, I cannot help thinking that God has abandoned it to some malignant being. I always except El Dorado. I scarce ever knew a city that did not wish the destruction of its neighboring city; nor a family that did not desire to exterminate some other family. The poor in all parts of the world bear an inveterate hatred to the rich, even while they creep and cringe to them; and the rich treat the poor like sheep, whose wool and flesh they barter for money; a million of regimented assassins traverse Europe from one end to the other, to get their bread by regular depredation and murder, because it is the most gentlemanlike profession. Even in those cities which seem to enjoy the blessings of peace, and where the arts flourish, the inhabitants are devoured with envy, care, and inquietudes, which are greater plagues than any experienced in a town besieged. Private chagrins are still more dreadful than public calamities. In a word," concluded the philosopher, "I have seen and suffered so much that I am a Manichaean."

"And yet there is some good in the world," replied Candide.

"Maybe so," said Martin, "but it has escaped my knowledge."

While they were deeply engaged in this dispute they heard the report of cannon, which redoubled every moment. Each took out his glass, and they spied two ships warmly engaged at the distance of about three miles. The wind brought them both so near the French ship that those on board her had the pleasure of seeing the fight with great ease.After several smart broadsides the one gave the other a shot between wind and water which sunk her outright. Then could Candide and Martin plainly perceive a hundred men on the deck of the vessel which was sinking, who, with hands uplifted to Heaven, sent forth piercing cries, and were in a moment swallowed up by the waves.

"Well," said Martin, "you now see in what manner mankind treat one another."

"It is certain," said Candide, "that there is something diabolical in this affair." As he was speaking thus he spied something of a shining red hue, which swam close to the vessel. The boat was hoisted out to see what it might be, when it proved to be one of his sheep. Candide felt more joy at the recovery of this one animal than he did grief when he lost the other hundred, though laden with the large diamonds of El Dorado.

The French captain quickly perceived that the victorious ship belonged to the crown of Spain; that the other was a Dutch pirate, and the very same captain who had robbed Candide. The immense riches which this villain had amassed, were buried with him in the deep, and only this one sheep saved out of the whole.

"You see," said Candide to Martin, "that vice is sometimes punished.This villain, the Dutch skipper, has met with the fate he deserved."

"Very true," said Martin, "but why should the passengers be doomed also to destruction? God has punished the knave, and the Devil has drowned the rest."

The French and Spanish ships continued their cruise, and Candide and Martin their conversation. They disputed fourteen days successively, at the end of which they were just as far advanced as the first moment they began. However, they had the satisfaction of disputing, of communicating their ideas, and of mutually comforting each other.Candide embraced his sheep with transport.

"Since I have found thee again," said he, "I may possibly find my Cunegund once more."

CHAPTER 21

Candide and Martin, While Thus Reasoning with Each Other, Draw Near to the Coast of France

At length they descried the coast of France, when Candide said to Martin, "Pray Monsieur Martin, were you ever in France?"

"Yes, sir," said Martin, "I have been in several provinces of that kingdom. In some, one half of the people are fools and madmen; in some, they are too artful; in others, again, they are, in general, either very good–natured or very brutal; while in others, they affect to be witty, and in all, their ruling passion is love, the next is slander, and the last is to talk nonsense."

"But, pray, Monsieur Martin, were you ever in Paris?"

"Yes, sir, I have been in that city, and it is a place that contains the several species just described; it is a chaos, a confused multitude, where everyone seeks for pleasure without being able to find it; at least, as far as I have observed during my short stay in that city. At my arrival I was robbed of all I had in the world by pickpockets and sharpers, at the fair of Saint–Germain. I was taken up myself for a robber, and confined in prison a whole week; after which I hired myself as corrector to a press in order to get a little money towards defraying my expenses back to Holland on foot.I knew the whole tribe of scribblers, malcontents, and fanatics. It is said the people of that city are very polite; I believe they may be."

"For my part, I have no curiosity to see France," said Candide. "You may easily conceive, my friend, that after spending a month in El Dorado, I can desire to behold nothing upon earth but Miss Cunegund. I am going to wait for her at Venice. I intend to pass through France, on my way to Italy. Will you not bear me company?"

"With all my heart," said Martin. "They say Venice is agreeable to none but noble Venetians, but that, nevertheless, strangers are well received there when they have plenty of money; now I have none, but you have, therefore I will attend you wherever you please."

"Now we are upon this subject," said Candide, "do you think that the earth was originally sea, as we read in that great book which belongs to the captain of the ship?"

"I believe nothing of it," replied Martin, "any more than I do of the many other chimeras which have been related to us for some time past."

"But then, to what end," said Candide, "was the world formed?"

"To make us mad," said Martin.

"Are you not surprised," continued Candide, "at the love which the two girls in the country of the Oreillons had for those two monkeys? – You know I have told you the story."

"Surprised?" replied Martin, "not in the least. I see nothing strange in this passion. I have seen so many extraordinary things that there is nothing extraordinary to me now."

"Do you think," said Candide, "that mankind always massacred one another as they do now? Were they always guilty of lies, fraud, treachery, ingratitude, inconstancy, envy, ambition, and cruelty? Were they always thieves, fools, cowards, gluttons, drunkards, misers, calumniators, debauchees, fanatics, and hypocrites?"

"Do you believe," said Martin, "that hawks have always been accustomed to eat pigeons when they came in their way?"

"Doubtless," said Candide.

"Well then," replied Martin, "if hawks have always had the same nature, why should you pretend that mankind change theirs?"

"Oh," said Candide, "there is a great deal of difference; for free will –" and reasoning thus they arrived at Bordeaux.

CHAPTER 22

What Happened to Candide and Martin in France

Candide stayed no longer at Bordeaux than was necessary to dispose of a few of the pebbles he had brought from El Dorado, and to provide himself with a post–chaise for two persons, for he could no longer stir a step without his philosopher Martin. The only thing that give him concern was being obliged to leave his sheep behind him, which he intrusted to the care of the Academy of Sciences at Bordeaux, who proposed, as a prize subject for the year, to prove why the wool of this sheep was red; and the prize was adjudged to a northern sage, who demonstrated by A plus B, minus C, divided by Z, that the sheep must necessarily be red, and die of the mange.

In the meantime, all travelers whom Candide met with in the inns, or on the road, told him to a man, that they were going to Paris. This general eagerness gave him likewise a great desire to see this capital; and it was not much out of his way to Venice.

He entered the city by the suburbs of Saint–Marceau, and thought himself in one of the vilest hamlets in all Westphalia.

Candide had not been long at his inn, before he was seized with a slight disorder, owing to the fatigue he had undergone. As he wore a diamond of an enormous size on his finger and had among the rest of his equipage a strong box that seemed very weighty, he soon found himself between two physicians, whom he had not sent for, a number of intimate friends whom he had never seen, and who would not quit his bedside, and two women devotees, who were very careful in providing him hot broths.

"I remember," said Martin to him, "that the first time I came to Paris I was likewise taken ill. I was very poor, and accordingly I had neither friends, nurses, nor physicians, and yet I did very well."

However, by dint of purging and bleeding, Candide's disorder became very serious. The priest of the parish came with all imaginable politeness to desire a note of him, payable to the bearer in the other world. Candide refused to comply with his request; but the two devotees assured him that it was a new fashion. Candide replied, that he was not one that followed the fashion. Martin was for throwing the priest out of the window. The clerk swore Candide should not have

Christian burial. Martin swore in his turn that he would bury the clerk alive if he continued to plague them any longer. The dispute grew warm; Martin took him by the shoulders and turned him out of the room, which gave great scandal, and occasioned a proces–verbal.

Candide recovered, and till he was in a condition to go abroad had a great deal of good company to pass the evenings with him in his chamber. They played deep. Candide was surprised to find he could never turn a trick; and Martin was not at all surprised at the matter.

Among those who did him the honors of the place was a little spruce abbe of Perigord, one of those insinuating, busy, fawning, impudent, necessary fellows, that lay wait for strangers on their arrival, tell them all the scandal of the town, and offer to minister to their pleasures at various prices. This man conducted Candide and Martin to the playhouse; they were acting a new tragedy.Candide found himself placed near a cluster of wits: this, however, did not prevent him from shedding tears at some parts of the piece which were most affecting, and best acted.

One of these talkers said to him between acts, "You are greatly to blame to shed tears; that actress plays horribly, and the man that plays with her still worse, and the piece itself is still more execrable than the representation. The author does not understand a word of Arabic, and yet he has laid his scene in Arabia, and what is more, he is a fellow who does not believe in innate ideas. Tomorrow I will bring you a score of pamphlets that have been written against him."

"Pray, sir," said Candide to the abbe, "how many theatrical pieces have you in France?"

"Five or six thousand," replied the abbe.

"Indeed! that is a great number," said Candide, "but how many good ones may there be?"

"About fifteen or sixteen."

"Oh! that is a great number," said Martin.

Candide was greatly taken with an actress, who performed the part of Queen Elizabeth in a dull kind of tragedy that is played sometimes.

"That actress," said he to Martin, "pleases me greatly; she has some sort of resemblance to Miss Cunegund. I should be very glad to pay my respects to her."

The abbe of Perigord offered his service to introduce him to her at her own house. Candide, who was brought up in Germany, desired to know what might be the ceremonial used on those occasions, and how a queen of England was treated in France.

"There is a necessary distinction to be observed in these matters," said the abbe. "In a country town we take them to a tavern; here in Paris, they are treated with great respect during their lifetime, provided they are handsome, and when they die we throw their bodies upon a dunghill."

"How?" said Candide, "throw a queen's body upon a dunghill!"

"The gentleman is quite right," said Martin, "he tells you nothing but the truth. I happened to be at Paris when Miss Monimia made her exit, as one may say, out of this world into another. She was refused what they call here the rites of sepulture; that is to say, she was denied the privilege of rotting in a churchyard by the side of all the beggars in the parish. They buried her at the corner of Burgundy Street, which must certainly have shocked her extremely, as she had very exalted notions of things."

"This is acting very impolitely," said Candide.

"Lord!" said Martin, "what can be said to it? It is the way of these people. Figure to yourself all the contradictions, all the inconsistencies possible, and you may meet with them in the government, the courts of justice, the churches, and the public spectacles of this odd nation."

"Is it true," said Candide, "that the people of Paris are always laughing?"

"Yes," replied the abbe, "but it is with anger in their hearts; they express all their complaints by loud bursts of laughter, and commit the most detestable crimes with a smile on their faces."

"Who was that great overgrown beast," said Candide, "who spoke so ill to me of the piece with which I was so much affected, and of the players who gave me so much pleasure?"

"A very good–for–nothing sort of a man I assure you," answered the abbe, "one who gets his livelihood by abusing every new book and play that is written or performed; he dislikes much to see anyone meet with success, like eunuchs, who detest everyone that possesses those powers they are deprived of; he is one of those vipers in literature who nourish themselves with their own venom; a pamphlet–monger."

"A pamphlet–monger!" said Candide, "what is that?"

"Why, a pamphlet–monger," replied the abbe, "is a writer of pamphlets – a fool."

Candide, Martin, and the abbe of Perigord argued thus on the staircase, while they stood to see the people go out of the playhouse.

"Though I am very anxious to see Miss Cunegund again," said Candide, "yet I have a great inclination to sup with Miss Clairon, for I am really much taken with her."

The abbe was not a person to show his face at this lady's house, which was frequented by none but the best company.

"She is engaged this evening," said he, "but I will do myself the honor to introduce you to a lady of quality of my acquaintance, at whose house you will see as much of the manners of Paris as if you had lived here for forty years."

Candide, who was naturally curious, suffered himself to be conducted to this lady's house, which was in the suburbs of Saint–Honore. The company was engaged at basser; twelve melancholy punters held each in his hand a small pack of cards, the corners of which were doubled down, and were so many registers of their ill fortune. A profound silence reigned throughout the assembly, a pallid dread had taken possession of the countenances of the punters, and restless inquietude stretched every muscle of the face of him who kept the bank; and the lady of the house, who was seated next to him, observed with lynx's eyes every play made, and noted those who tallied, and made them undouble their cards with a severe exactness, though mixed with a politeness, which she thought necessary not to frighten away her customers. This lady assumed the title of Marchioness of Parolignac.Her daughter, a girl of about fifteen years of age, was one of the punters, and took care to give her mamma a hint, by signs, when any one of the players attempted to repair the rigor of their ill fortune by a little innocent deception. The company were thus occupied when Candide, Martin, and the abbe made their entrance; not a creature rose to salute them, or indeed took the least notice of them, being wholly intent upon the business at hand.

"Ah!" said Candide, "My Lady Baroness of Thunder–ten–tronckh would have behaved more civilly."

However, the abbe whispered in the ear of the Marchioness, who half raising herself from her seat, honored Candide with a gracious smile, and gave Martin a nod of her head, with an air of inexpressible dignity. She then ordered a seat for Candide, and desired him to make one of their party at play; he did so, and in a few deals lost near a thousand pieces; after which they supped very elegantly, and everyone was surprised at seeing Candide lose so much money without appearing to be the least disturbed at it. The servants in waiting said to each other, "This is certainly some English lord."

The supper was like most others of its kind in Paris. At first everyone was silent; then followed a few confused murmurs, and afterwards several insipid jokes passed and repassed, with false reports, false reasonings, a little politics, and a great deal of scandal. The conversation then turned upon the new productions in literature.

"Pray," said the abbe, "good folks, have you seen the romance written by a certain Gauchat, Doctor of Divinity?"

"Yes," answered one of the company, "but I had not patience to go through it. The town is pestered with a swarm of impertinent productions, but this of Dr. Gauchat's outdoes them all. In short, I was so cursedly tired of reading this vile stuff that I even resolved to come here, and make a party at basset."

"But what say you to the archdeacon T–'s miscellaneous collection," said the abbe.

"Oh my God!" cried the Marchioness of Parolignac, "never mention the tedious creature! Only think what pains he is at to tell one things that all the world knows; and how he labors an argument that is hardly worth the slightest consideration! how absurdly he makes use of other people's wit! how miserably he mangles what he has pilfered from them! The man makes me quite sick! A few pages of the good archdeacon are enough in conscience to satisfy anyone."

There was at the table a person of learning and taste, who supported what the Marchioness had advanced. They next began to talk of tragedies. The lady desired to know how it came about that there were several tragedies, which still continued to be played, though they would not bear reading? The man of taste explained very clearly how a piece may be in some manner interesting without having a grain of merit. He showed, in a few words, that it is not sufficient to throw together a few incidents that are to be met with in every romance, and that to dazzle the spectator the thoughts should be new, without being farfetched; frequently sublime, but always natural; the author should have a thorough knowledge of the human heart and make it speak properly; he should be a complete poet, without showing an affectation of it in any of the characters of his piece; he should be a perfect master of his language, speak it with all its purity, and with the utmost harmony, and yet so as not to make the sense a slave to the rhyme.

"Whoever," added he, "neglects any one of these rules, though he may write two or three tragedies with tolerable success, will never be reckoned in the number of good authors. There are very few good tragedies; some are idylls, in very well–written and harmonious dialogue; and others a chain of political reasonings that set one asleep, or else pompous and high–flown amplification, that disgust rather than please. Others again are the ravings of a madman, in an uncouth style, unmeaning flights, or long apostrophes to the deities, for want of knowing how to address mankind; in a word a collection of false maxims and dull commonplace."

Candide listened to this discourse with great attention, and conceived a high opinion of the person who delivered it; and as the Marchioness had taken care to place him near her side, he took the liberty to whisper her softly in the ear and ask who this person was that spoke so well.

"He is a man of letters," replied Her Ladyship, "who never plays, and whom the abbe brings with him to my house sometimes to spend an evening. He is a great judge of writing, especially in tragedy; he has composed one himself, which was damned, and has written a book that was never seen out of his bookseller's shop, excepting only one copy, which he sent me with a dedication, to which he had prefixed my name."

"Oh the great man," cried Candide, "he is a second Pangloss."

Then turning towards him, "Sir," said he, "you are doubtless of opinion that everything is for the best in the physical and moral world, and that nothing could be otherwise than it is?"

"I, sir!" replied the man of letters, "I think no such thing, I assure you; I find that all in this world is set the wrong end uppermost. No one knows what is his rank, his office, nor what he does, nor what he should do. With the exception of our evenings, which we generally pass tolerably merrily, the rest of our time is spent in idle disputes and quarrels, Jansenists against Molinists, the Parliament against the Church, and one armed body of men against another; courtier against courtier, husband against wife, and relations against relations. In short, this world is nothing but one continued scene of civil war."

"Yes," said Candide, "and I have seen worse than all that; and yet a learned man, who had the misfortune to be hanged, taught me that everything was marvelously well, and that these evils you are speaking of were only so many shades in a beautiful picture."

"Your hempen sage," said Martin, "laughed at you; these shades, as you call them, are most horrible blemishes."

"The men make these blemishes," rejoined Candide, "and they cannot do otherwise."

"Then it is not their fault," added Martin.

The greatest part of the gamesters, who did not understand a syllable of this discourse, amused themselves with drinking, while Martin reasoned with the learned gentleman and Candide entertained the lady of the house with a part of his adventures.

After supper the Marchioness conducted Candide into her dressingroom, and made him sit down under a canopy.

"Well," said she, "are you still so violently fond of Miss Cunegund of Thunder–ten–tronckh?"

"Yes, madam," replied Candide.

The Marchioness said to him with a tender smile, "You answer me like a young man born in Westphalia; a Frenchman would have said, 'It is true, madam, I had a great passion for Miss Cunegund; but since I have seen you, I fear I can no longer love her as I did.'"

"Alas! madam," replied Candide, "I will make you what answer you please."

"You fell in love with her, I find, in stooping to pick up her handkerchief which she had dropped; you shall pick up my garter."

"With all my heart, madam," said Candide, and he picked it up.

"But you must tie it on again," said the lady.

Candide tied it on again.

"Look ye, young man," said the Marchioness, "you are a stranger; I make some of my lovers here in Paris languish for me a whole fortnight; but I surrender to you at first sight, because I am willing to do the honors of my country to a young Westphalian."

The fair one having cast her eye on two very large diamonds that were upon the young stranger's finger, praised them in so earnest a manner that they were in an instant transferred from his finger to hers.

As Candide was going home with the abbe he felt some qualms of conscience for having been guilty of infidelity to Miss Cunegund.The abbe took part with him in his uneasiness; he had but an inconsiderable share in the thousand pieces Candide had lost at play, and the two diamonds which had been in a manner extorted from him; and therefore very prudently designed to make the most he could of his new acquaintance, which chance had thrown in his way. He talked much of Miss Cunegund, and Candide assured him that he would heartily ask pardon of that fair one for his infidelity to her, when he saw her at Venice.

The abbe redoubled his civilities and seemed to interest himself warmly in everything that Candide said, did, or seemed inclined to do.

"And so, sir, you have an engagement at Venice?"

"Yes, Monsieur l'Abbe," answered Candide, "I must absolutely wait upon Miss Cunegund," and then the pleasure he took in talking about the object he loved, led him insensibly to relate, according to custom, part of his adventures with that illustrious Westphalian beauty.

"I fancy," said the abbe, "Miss Cunegund has a great deal of wit, and that her letters must be very entertaining."

"I never received any from her," said Candide; "for you are to consider that, being expelled from the castle upon her account, I could not write to her, especially as soon after my departure I heard she was dead; but thank God I found afterwards she was living. I left her again after this, and now I have sent a messenger to her near two thousand leagues from here, and wait here for his return with an answer from her."

The artful abbe let not a word of all this escape him, though he seemed to be musing upon something else. He soon took his leave of the two adventurers, after having embraced them with the greatest cordiality.

The next morning, almost as soon as his eyes were open, Candide received the following billet:

"My Dearest Lover – I have been ill in this city these eight days.I have heard of your arrival, and should fly to your arms were I able to stir. I was informed of your being on the way hither at Bordeaux, where I left the faithful Cacambo, and the old woman, who will soon follow me. The Governor of Buenos Ayres has taken everything from me but your heart, which I still retain. Come to me immediately on the receipt of this. Your presence will either give me new life, or kill me with the pleasure."

At the receipt of this charming, this unexpected letter, Candide felt the utmost transports of joy; though, on the other hand, the indisposition of his beloved Miss Cunegund overwhelmed him with grief.Distracted between these two passions he took his gold and his diamonds, and procured a person to conduct him and Martin to the house where Miss Cunegund lodged. Upon entering the room he felt his limbs tremble, his heart flutter, his tongue falter; he attempted to undraw the curtain, and called for a light to the bedside.

"Lord sir," cried a maidservant, who was waiting in the room, "take care what you do, Miss cannot bear the least light," and so saying she pulled the curtain close again.

"Cunegund! my dear cried Candide, bathed in tears, "how do you do?If you cannot bear the light, speak to me at least."

"Alas! she cannot speak," said the maid.

The sick lady then put a plump hand out of the bed and Candide first bathed it with tears, then filled it with diamonds, leaving a purse of gold upon the easy chair.

In the midst of his transports came an officer into the room, followed by the abbe, and a file of musketeers.

"There," said he, "are the two suspected foreigners." At the same time he ordered them to be seized and carried to prison.

"Travelers are not treated in this manner in the country of El Dorado," said Candide.

"I am more of a Manichaean now than ever," said Martin.

"But pray, good sir, where are you going to carry us?" said Candide.

"To a dungeon, my dear sir," replied the officer.

When Martin had a little recovered himself, so as to form a cool judgment of what had passed, he plainly perceived that the person who had acted the part of Miss Cunegund was a cheat; that the abbe of Perigord was a sharper who had imposed upon the honest simplicity of Candide, and that the officer was a knave, whom they might easily get rid of.

Candide following the advice of his friend Martin, and burning with impatience to see the real Miss Cunegund, rather than be obliged to appear at a court of justice, proposed to the officer to make him a present of three small diamonds, each of them worth three thousand pistoles.

"Ah, sir," said the understrapper of justice, "had you commited ever so much villainy, this would render you the honestest man living, in my eyes. Three diamonds worth three thousand pistoles! Why, my dear sir, so far from carrying you to jail, I would lose my life to serve you. There are orders for stopping all strangers; but leave it to me, I have a brother at Dieppe, in Normandy. I myself will conduct you thither, and if you have a diamond left to give him he will take as much care of you as I myself should."

"But why," said Candide, "do they stop all strangers?"

The abbe of Perigord made answer that it was because a poor devil of the country of Atrebata heard somebody tell foolish stories, and this induced him to commit a parricide; not such a one as that in the month of May, 1610, but such as that in the month of December in the year 1594, and such as many that have been perpetrated in other months and years, by other poor devils who had heard foolish stories.

The officer then explained to them what the abbe meant.

"Horrid monsters," exclaimed Candide, "is it possible that such scenes should pass among a people who are perpetually singing and dancing? Is there no flying this abominable country immediately, this execrable kingdom where monkeys provoke tigers? I have seen bears in my country, but men I have beheld nowhere but in El Dorado. In the name of God, sir," said he to the officer, "do me the kindness to conduct me to Venice, where I am to wait for Miss Cunegund."

"Really, sir," replied the officer, "I cannot possibly wait on you farther than Lower Normandy."

So saying, he ordered Candide's irons to be struck off, acknowledged himself mistaken, and sent his followers about their business, after which he conducted Candide and Martin to Dieppe, and left them to the care of his brother.

There happened just then to be a small Dutch ship in the harbor. The Norman, whom the other three diamonds had converted into the most obliging, serviceable being that ever breathed, took care to see Candide and his attendants safe on board this vessel, that was just ready to sail for Portsmouth in England. This was not the nearest way to Venice, indeed, but Candide thought himself escaped out of Hell, and did not, in the least, doubt but he should quickly find an opportunity of resuming his voyage to Venice.

CHAPTER 23

Candide and Martin Touch upon the English Coast – What They See There

Ah Pangloss! Pangloss! ah Martin! ah my dear Miss Cunegund! What sort of a world is this?" Thus exclaimed Candide as soon as he got on board the Dutch ship.

"Why something very foolish, and very abominable," said Martin.

"You are acquainted with England," said Candide; "are they as great fools in that country as in France?"

"Yes, but in a different manner," answered Martin. "You know that these two nations are at war about a few acres of barren land in the neighborhood of Canada, and that they have expended much greater sums in the contest than all Canada is worth. To say exactly whether there are a greater number fit to be inhabitants of a madhouse in the one country than the other, exceeds the limits of my imperfect capacity; I know in general that the people we are going to visit are of a very dark and gloomy disposition."

As they were chatting thus together they arrived at Portsmouth.The shore on each side the harbor was lined with a multitude of people, whose eyes were steadfastly fixed on a lusty man who was kneeling down on the deck of one of the men–of–war, with something tied before his eyes. Opposite to this personage stood four soldiers, each of whom shot three bullets into his skull, with all the composure imaginable; and when it was done, the whole company went away perfectly well satisfied.

"What the devil is all this for?" said Candide, "and what demon, or foe of mankind, lords it thus tyrannically over the world?"

He then asked who was that lusty man who had been sent out of the world with so much ceremony. When he received for answer, that it was an admiral.

"And pray why do you put your admiral to death?"

"Because he did not put a sufficient number of his fellow creatures to death. You must know, he had an engagement with a French admiral, and it has been proved against him that he was not near enough to his antagonist."

"But," replied Candide, "the French admiral must have been as far from him."

"There is no doubt of that; but in this country it is found requisite, now and then, to put an admiral to death, in order to encourage the others to fight."

Candide was so shocked at what he saw and heard, that he would not set foot on shore, but made a bargain with the Dutch skipper (were he even to rob him like the captain of Surinam) to carry him directly to Venice.

The skipper was ready in two days. They sailed along the coast of France, and passed within sight of Lisbon, at which Candide trembled. From thence they proceeded to the Straits, entered the Mediterranean, and at length arrived at Venice.

"God be praised," said Candide, embracing Martin, "this is the place where I am to behold my beloved Cunegund once again. I can confide in Cacambo, like another self. All is well, all is very well, all is well as possible."

CHAPTER 24

Of Pacquette and Friar Giroflee

Upon their arrival at Venice Candide went in search of Cacambo at every inn and coffee–house, and among all the ladies of pleasure, but could hear nothing of him. He sent every day to inquire what ships were in, still no news of Cacambo.

"It is strange," said he to Martin, "very strange that I should have time to sail from Surinam to Bordeaux; to travel thence to Paris, to Dieppe, to Portsmouth; to sail along the coast of Portugal and Spain, and up the Mediterranean to spend some months at Venice; and that my lovely Cunegund should not have arrived. Instead of her, I only met with a Parisian impostor, and a rascally abbe of Perigord.Cunegund is actually dead, and I have nothing to do but follow her.Alas! how much better would it have been for me to have remained in the paradise of El Dorado than to have returned to this cursed Europe!You are in the right, my dear Martin; you are certainly in the right; all is misery and deceit."

He fell into a deep melancholy, and neither went to the opera then in vogue, nor partook of any of the diversions of the Carnival; nay, he even slighted the fair sex.

Martin said to him, "Upon my word, I think you are very simple to imagine that a rascally valet, with five or six millions in his pocket, would go in search of your mistress to the further of the world, and bring her to Venice to meet you. If he finds her he will take her for himself; if he does not, he will take another. Let me advise you to forget your valet Cacambo, and your mistress Cunegund."

Martin's speech was not the most consolatory to the dejected Candide. His melancholy increased, and Martin never ceased trying to prove to him that there is very little virtue or happiness in this world; except, perhaps, in El Dorado, where hardly anybody can gain admittance.

While they were disputing on this important subject, and still expecting Miss Cunegund, Candide perceived a young Theatin friar in the Piazza San Marco, with a girl under his arm. The Theatin looked fresh–colored, plump, and vigorous; his eyes sparkled; his air and gait were bold and lofty. The girl was pretty, and was singing a song; and every now and then gave her Theatin an amorous ogle and wantonly pinched his ruddy cheeks.

"You will at least allow," said Candide to Martin, "that these two are happy. Hitherto I have met with none but unfortunate people in the whole habitable globe, except in El Dorado; but as to this couple, I would venture to lay a wager they are happy."

"Done!" said Martin, "they are not what you imagine."

"Well, we have only to ask them to dine with us," said Candide, "and you will see whether I am mistaken or not."

Thereupon he accosted them, and with great politeness invited them to his inn to eat some macaroni, with Lombard partridges and caviar, and to drink a bottle of Montepulciano, Lacryma Christi, Cyprus, and Samos wine. The girl blushed; the Theatin accepted the invitation and she followed him, eyeing Candide every now and then with a mixture of surprise and confusion, while the tears stole down her cheeks. No sooner did she enter his apartment than she cried out, "How, Monsieur Candide, have you quite forgot your Pacquette? do you not know her again?"

Candide had not regarded her with any degree of attention before, being wholly occupied with the thoughts of his dear Cunegund.

"Ah! is it you, child? was it you that reduced Dr. Pangloss to that fine condition I saw him in?"

"Alas! sir," answered Pacquette, "it was I, indeed. I find you are acquainted with everything; and I have been informed of all the misfortunes that happened to the whole family of My Lady Baroness and the fair Cunegund. But I can safely swear to you that my lot was no less deplorable; I was innocence itself when you saw me last. A Franciscan, who was my confessor, easily seduced me; the consequences proved terrible. I was obliged to leave the castle some time after the Baron kicked you out by the backside from there; and if a famous surgeon had not taken compassion on me, I had been a dead woman. Gratitude obliged me to live with him some time as his mistress; his wife, who was a very devil for jealousy, beat me unmercifully every day. Oh! she was a perfect fury. The doctor himself was the most ugly of all mortals, and I the most wretched creature existing, to be continually beaten for a man whom I did not love.You are sensible, sir, how dangerous it was for an ill–natured woman to be married to a physician. Incensed at the behavior of his wife, he one day gave her so affectionate a remedy for a slight cold she had caught that she died in less than two hours in most dreadful convulsions. Her relations prosecuted the husband, who was obliged to fly, and I was sent to prison. My innocence would not have saved me, if I had not been tolerably handsome. The judge gave me my liberty on condition he should succeed the doctor. However, I was soon supplanted by a rival, turned off without a farthing, and obliged to continue the abominable trade which you men think so pleasing, but which to us unhappy creatures is the most dreadful of all sufferings. At length I came to follow the business at Venice. Ah!sir, did you but know what it is to be obliged to receive every visitor; old tradesmen, counselors, monks, watermen, and abbes; to be exposed to all their insolence and abuse; to be often necessitated to borrow a petticoat, only that it may be taken up by some disagreeable wretch; to be robbed by one gallant of what we get from another; to be subject to the extortions of civil magistrates; and to have forever before one's eyes the prospect of old age, a hospital, or a dunghill, you would conclude that I am one of the most unhappy wretches breathing."

Thus did Pacquette unbosom herself to honest Candide in his closet, in the presence of Martin, who took occasion to say to him, "You see I have half won the wager already."

Friar Giroflee was all this time in the parlor refreshing himself with a glass or two of wine till dinner was ready.

"But," said Candide to Pacquette, "you looked so gay and contented, when I met you, you sang and caressed the Theatin with so much fondness, that I absolutely thought you as happy as you say you are now miserable."

"Ah! dear sir," said Pacquette, "this is one of the miseries of the trade; yesterday I was stripped and beaten by an officer; yet today I must appear good humored and gay to please a friar."

Candide was convinced and acknowledged that Martin was in the right.They sat down to table with Pacquette and the Theatin; the entertainment was agreeable, and towards the end they began to converse together with some freedom.

"Father," said Candide to the friar, "you seem to me to enjoy a state of happiness that even kings might envy; joy and health are painted in your countenance. You have a pretty wench to divert you; and you seem to be perfectly well contented with your condition as a Theatin."

"Faith, sir," said Friar Giroflee, "I wish with all my soul the Theatins were every one of them at the bottom of the sea. I have been tempted a thousand times to set fire to the monastery and go and turn Turk. My parents obliged me, at the age of fifteen, to put on this detestable habit only to increase the fortune of an elder brother of mine, whom God confound! jealousy, discord, and fury, reside in our monastery. It is true I have preached often paltry sermons, by which I have got a little money, part of which the prior robs me of, and the remainder helps to pay my girls; but, not withstanding, at night, when I go hence to my monastery, I am ready to dash my brains against the walls of the dormitory; and this is the case with all the rest of our fraternity."

Martin, turning towards Candide, with his usual indifference, said, "Well, what think you now? have I won the wager entirely?"

Candide gave two thousand piastres to Pacquette, and a thousand to Friar Giroflee, saying, "I will answer that this will make them happy."

"I am not of your opinion," said Martin, "perhaps this money will only make them wretched."

"Be that as it may," said Candide, "one thing comforts me; I see that one often meets with those whom one never expected to see again; so that, perhaps, as I have found my red sheep and Pacquette, I may be lucky enough to find Miss Cunegund also."

"I wish," said Martin, "she one day may make you happy; but I doubt it much."

"You lack faith," said Candide.

"It is because," said Martin, "I have seen the world."

"Observe those gondoliers," said Candide, "are they not perpetually singing?"

"You do not see them," answered Martin, "at home with their wives and brats. The doge has his chagrin, gondoliers theirs.Nevertheless, in the main, I look upon the gondolier's life as preferable to that of the doge; but the difference is so trifling that it is not worth the trouble of examining into."

"I have heard great talk," said Candide, "of the Senator Pococurante, who lives in that fine house at the Brenta, where, they say, he entertains foreigners in the most polite manner."

"They pretend this man is a perfect stranger to uneasiness. I should be glad to see so extraordinary a being," said Martin.

Candide thereupon sent a messenger to Seignor Pococurante, desiring permission to wait on him the next day.

CHAPTER 25

Candide and Martin Pay a Visit to Seignor Pococurante, a Noble Venetian

Candide and his friend Martin went in a gondola on the Brenta, and arrived at the palace of the noble Pococurante. The gardens were laid out in elegant taste, and adorned with fine marble statues; his palace was built after the most approved rules of architecture. The master of the house, who was a man of affairs, and very rich, received our two travelers with great politeness, but without much ceremony, which somewhat disconcerted Candide, but was not at all displeasing to Martin.

As soon as they were seated, two very pretty girls, neatly dressed, brought in chocolate, which was extremely well prepared.Candide could not help praising their beauty and graceful carriage.

"The creatures are all right," said the senator; "I amuse myself with them sometimes, for I am heartily tired of the women of the town, their coquetry, their jealousy, their quarrels, their humors, their meannesses, their pride, and their folly; I am weary of making sonnets, or of paying for sonnets to be made on them; but after all, these two girls begin to grow very indifferent to me."

After having refreshed himself, Candide walked into a large gallery, where he was struck with the sight of a fine collection of paintings.

"Pray," said Candide, "by what master are the two first of these?"

"They are by Raphael," answered the senator. "I gave a great deal of money for them seven years ago, purely out of curiosity, as they were said to be the finest pieces in Italy; but I cannot say they please me: the coloring is dark and heavy; the figures do not swell nor come out enough; and the drapery is bad. In short, notwithstanding the encomiums lavished upon them, they are not, in my opinion, a true representation of nature. I approve of no paintings save those wherein I think I behold nature itself; and there are few, if any, of that kind to be met with. I have what is called a fine collection, but I take no manner of delight in it."

While dinner was being prepared Pococurante ordered a concert.Candide praised the music to the skies.

"This noise," said the noble Venetian, "may amuse one for a little time, but if it were to last above half an hour, it would grow tiresome to everybody, though perhaps no one would care to own it.Music has become the art of executing what is difficult; now, whatever is difficult cannot be long pleasing.

"I believe I might take more pleasure in an opera, if they had not made such a monster of that species of dramatic entertainment as perfectly shocks me; and I am amazed how people can bear to see wretched tragedies set to music; where the scenes are contrived for no other purpose than to lug in, as it were by the ears, three or four ridiculous songs, to give a favorite actress an opportunity of exhibiting her pipe. Let who will die away in raptures at the trills of a eunuch quavering the majestic part of Caesar or Cato, and strutting in a foolish manner upon the stage, but for my part I have long ago renounced these paltry entertainments, which constitute the glory of modern Italy, and are so dearly purchased by crowned heads."

Candide opposed these sentiments; but he did it in a discreet manner; as for Martin, he was entirely of the old senator's opinion.

Dinner being served they sat down to table, and, after a hearty repast, returned to the library. Candide, observing Homer richly bound, commended the noble Venetian's taste.

"This," said he, "is a book that was once the delight of the great Pangloss, the best philosopher in Germany."

"Homer is no favorite of mine," answered Pococurante, coolly, "I was made to believe once that I took a pleasure in reading him; but his continual repetitions of battles have all such a resemblance with each other; his gods that are forever in haste and bustle, without ever doing anything; his Helen, who is the cause of the war, and yet hardly acts in the whole performance; his Troy, that holds out so long, without being taken: in short, all these things together make the poem very insipid to me. I have asked some learned men, whether they are not in reality as much tired as myself with reading this poet: those who spoke ingenuously, assured me that he had made them fall asleep, and yet that they could not well avoid giving him a place in their libraries; but that it was merely as they would do an antique, or those rusty medals which are kept only for curiosity, and are of no manner of use in commerce."

"But your excellency does not surely form the same opinion of Virgil?" said Candide.

"Why, I grant," replied Pococurante, "that the second, third, fourth, and sixth books of his Aeneid, are excellent; but as for his pious Aeneas, his strong Cloanthus, his friendly Achates, his boy Ascanius, his silly king Latinus, his ill–bred Amata, his insipid Lavinia, and some other characters much in the same strain, I think there cannot in nature be anything more flat and disagreeable. I must confess I prefer Tasso far beyond him; nay, even that sleepy taleteller Ariosto."

"May I take the liberty to ask if you do not experience great pleasure from reading Horace?" said Candide.

"There are maxims in this writer," replied Pococurante, "whence a man of the world may reap some benefit; and the short measure of the verse makes them more easily to be retained in the memory. But I see nothing extraordinary in his journey to Brundusium, and his account of his had dinner; nor in his dirty, low quarrel between one Rupillius, whose words, as he expresses it, were full of poisonous filth; and another, whose language was dipped in vinegar. His indelicate verses against old women and witches have frequently given me great offense: nor can I discover the great merit of his telling his friend Maecenas, that if he will but rank him in the class of lyric poets, his lofty head shall touch the stars. Ignorant readers are apt to judge a writer by his reputation. For my part, I read only to please myself. I like nothing but what makes for my purpose."

Candide, who had been brought up with a notion of never making use of his own judgment, was astonished at what he heard; but Martin found there was a good deal of reason in the senator's remarks.

"Oh! here is a Tully," said Candide; "this great man I fancy you are never tired of reading?"

"Indeed I never read him at all," replied Pococurante. "What is it to me whether he pleads for Rabirius or Cluentius? I try causes enough myself. I had once some liking for his philosophical works; but when I found he doubted everything, I thought I knew as much as himself, and had no need of a guide to learn ignorance."

"Ha!" cried Martin, "here are fourscore volumes of the memoirs of the Academy of Sciences; perhaps there may be something curious and valuable in this collection."

"Yes," answered Pococurante, "so there might if any one of these compilers of this rubbish had only invented the art of pin–making; but all these volumes are filled with mere chimerical systems, without one single article conductive to real utility."

"I see a prodigious number of plays," said Candide, "in Italian, Spanish, and French."

"Yes," replied the Venetian, "there are I think three thousand, and not three dozen of them good for anything. As to those huge volumes of divinity, and those enormous collections of sermons, they are not all together worth one single page in Seneca; and I fancy you will readily believe that neither myself, nor anyone else, ever looks into them."

Martin, perceiving some shelves filled with English books, said to the senator, "I fancy that a republican must be highly delighted with those books, which are most of them written with a noble spirit of freedom."

"It is noble to write as we think," said Pococurante; "it is the privilege of humanity. Throughout Italy we write only what we do not think; and the present inhabitants of the country of the Caesars and Antonines dare not acquire a single idea without the permission of a Dominican father. I should be enamored of the spirit of the English nation, did it not utterly frustrate the good effects it would produce by passion and the spirit of party."

Candide, seeing a Milton, asked the senator if he did not think that author a great man.

"Who?" said Pococurante sharply; "that barbarian who writes a tedious commentary in ten books of rumbling verse, on the first chapter of Genesis? that slovenly imitator of the Greeks, who disfigures the creation, by making the Messiah take a pair of compasses from Heaven's armory to plan the world; whereas Moses represented the Diety as producing the whole universe by his fiat? Can I think you have any esteem for a writer who has spoiled Tasso's Hell and the Devil; who transforms Lucifer sometimes into a toad, and at others into a pygmy; who makes him say the same thing over again a hundred times; who metamorphoses him into a school–divine; and who, by an absurdly serious imitation of Ariosto's comic invention of firearms, represents the devils and angels cannonading each other in Heaven? Neither I nor any other Italian can possibly take pleasure in such melancholy reveries; but the marriage of Sin and Death, and snakes issuing from the womb of the former, are enough to make any person sick that is not lost to all sense of delicacy. This obscene, whimsical, and disagreeable poem met with the neglect it deserved at its first publication; and I only treat the author now as he was treated in his own country by his contemporaries."

Candide was sensibly grieved at this speech, as he had a great respect for Homer, and was fond of Milton.

"Alas!" said he softly to Martin, "I am afraid this man holds our German poets in great contempt."

"There would be no such great harm in that," said Martin.

"O what a surprising man!" said Candide, still to himself; "what a prodigious genius is this Pococurante! nothing can please him."

After finishing their survey of the library, they went down into the garden, when Candide commended the several beauties that offered themselves to his view.

"I know nothing upon earth laid out in such had taste," said Pococurante; "everything about it is childish and trifling; but I shall have another laid out tomorrow upon a nobler plan."

As soon as our two travelers had taken leave of His Excellency, Candide said to Martin, "Well, I hope you will own that this man is the happiest of all mortals, for he is above everything he possesses."

"But do not you see," answered Martin, "that he likewise dislikes everything he possesses? It was an observation of Plato, long since, that those are not the best stomachs that reject, without distinction, all sorts of aliments."

"True," said Candide, "but still there must certainly be a pleasure in criticising everything, and in perceiving faults where others think they see beauties."

"That is," replied Martin, "there is a pleasure in having no pleasure."

"Well, well," said Candide, "I find that I shall be the only happy man at last, when I am blessed with the sight of my dear Cunegund."

"It is good to hope," said Martin.

In the meanwhile, days and weeks passed away, and no news of Cacambo. Candide was so overwhelmed with grief, that he did not reflect on the behavior of Pacquette and Friar Giroflee, who never stayed to return him thanks for the presents he had so generously made them.

CHAPTER 26

Candide and Martin Sup with Six Sharpers – Who They Were

One evening as Candide, with his attendant Martin, was going to sit down to supper with some foreigners who lodged in the same inn where they had taken up their quarters, a man with a face the color of soot came behind him, and taking him by the arm, said, "Hold yourself in readiness to go along with us; be sure you do not fail."

Upon this, turning about to see from whom these words came, he beheld Cacambo. Nothing but the sight of Miss Cunegund could have given him greater joy and surprise. He was almost beside himself, and embraced this dear friend.

"Cunegund!" said he, "Cunegund is come with you doubtless! Where, where is she? Carry me to her this instant, that I may die with joy in her presence."

"Cunegund is not here," answered Cacambo; "she is in Constantinople."

"Good heavens! in Constantinople! but no matter if she were in China, I would fly thither. Quick, quick, dear Cacambo, let us be gone."

"Soft and fair," said Cacambo, "stay till you have supped. I cannot at present stay to say anything more to you; I am a slave, and my master waits for me; I must go and attend him at table: but mum! say not a word, only get your supper, and hold yourself in readiness."

Candide, divided between joy and grief, charmed to have thus met with his faithful agent again, and surprised to hear he was a slave, his heart palpitating, his senses confused, but full of the hopes of recovering his dear Cunegund, sat down to table with Martin, who beheld all these scenes with great unconcern, and with six strangers, who had come to spend the Carnival at Venice.

Cacambo waited at table upon one of those strangers. When supper was nearly over, he drew near to his master, and whispered in his ear:

"Sire, Your Majesty may go when you please; the ship is ready"; and so saying he left the room.

The guests, surprised at what they had heard, looked at each other without speaking a word; when another servant drawing near to his master, in like manner said, "Sire, Your Majesty's post–chaise is at Padua, and the bark is ready." The master made him a sign, and he instantly withdrew.

The company all stared at each other again, and the general astonishment was increased. A third servant then approached another of the strangers, and said, "Sire, if Your Majesty will be advised by me, you will not make any longer stay in this place; I will go and get everything ready"; and instantly disappeared.

Candide and Martin then took it for granted that this was some of the diversions of the Carnival, and that these were characters in masquerade. Then a fourth domestic said to the fourth stranger, "Your Majesty may set off when you please"; saying which, he went away like the rest. A fifth valet said the same to a fifth master. But the sixth domestic spoke in a different style to the person on whom he waited, and who sat near to Candide.

"Troth, sir," said he, "they will trust Your Majesty no longer, nor myself neither; and we may both of us chance to be sent to jail this very night; and therefore I shall take care of myself, and so adieu."

The servants being all gone, the six strangers, with Candide and Martin, remained in a profound silence. At length Candide broke it by saying:

"Gentlemen, this is a very singular joke upon my word; how came you all to be kings? For my part I own frankly, that neither my friend Martin here, nor myself, have any claim to royalty."

Cacambo's master then began, with great gravity, to deliver himself thus in Italian:

"I am not joking in the least, my name is Achmet III. I was Grand Sultan for many years; I dethroned my brother, my nephew dethroned me, my viziers lost their heads, and I am condemned to end my days in the old seraglio. My nephew, the Grand Sultan Mahomet, gives me permission to travel sometimes for my health, and I am come to spend the Carnival at Venice."

A young man who sat by Achmet, spoke next, and said:

"My name is Ivan. I was once Emperor of all the Russians, but was dethroned in my cradle. My parents were confined, and I was brought up in a prison, yet I am sometimes allowed to travel, though always with persons to keep a guard over me, and I come to spend the Carnival at Venice."

The third said:

"I am Charles Edward, King of England; my father has renounced his right to the throne in my favor. I have fought in defense of my rights, and near a thousand of my friends have had their hearts taken out of their bodies alive and thrown in their faces. I have myself been confined in a prison. I am going to Rome to visit the King, my father, who was dethroned as well as myself; and my grandfather and I have come to spend the Carnival at Venice."

The fourth spoke thus:

"I am the King of Poland; the fortune of war has stripped me of my hereditary dominions. My father experienced the same vicissitudes of fate. I resign myself to the will of Providence, in the same manner as Sultan Achmet, the Emperor Ivan, and King Charles Edward, whom God long preserve; and I have come to spend the Carnival at Venice."

The fifth said:

"I am King of Poland also. I have twice lost my kingdom; but Providence has given me other dominions, where I have done more good than all the Sarmatian kings put together were ever able to do on the banks of the Vistula; I resign myself likewise to Providence; and have come to spend the Carnival at Venice."

It now came to the sixth monarch's turn to speak. "Gentlemen," said he, "I am not so great a prince as the rest of you, it is true, but I am, however, a crowned head. I am Theodore, elected King of Corsica. I have had the title of Majesty, and am now hardly treated with common civility. I have coined money, and am not now worth a single ducat. I have had two secretaries, and am now without a valet. I was once seated on a throne, and since that have lain upon a truss of straw, in a common jail in London, and I very much fear I shall meet with the same fate here in Venice, where I came, like Your Majesties, to divert myself at the Carnival."

The other five Kings listened to this speech with great attention; it excited their compassion; each of them made the unhappy Theodore a present of twenty sequins, and Candide gave him a diamond, worth just a hundred times that sum.

"Who can this private person be," said the five Kings to one another, "who is able to give, and has actually given, a hundred times as much as any of us?"

Just as they rose from table, in came four Serene Highnesses, who had also been stripped of their territories by the fortune of war, and had come to spend the remainder of the Carnival at Venice. Candide took no manner of notice of them; for his thoughts were wholly employed on his voyage to Constantinople, where he intended to go in search of his lovely Miss Cunegund.

CHAPTER 27

Candide's Voyage to Constantinople

The trusty Cacambo had already engaged the captain of the Turkish ship that was to carry Sultan Achmet back to Constantinople to take Candide and Martin on board. Accordingly they both embarked, after paying their obeisance to his miserable Highness. As they were going on board, Candide said to Martin:

"You see we supped in company with six dethroned Kings, and to one of them I gave charity. Perhaps there may be a great many other princes still more unfortunate. For my part I have lost only a hundred sheep, and am now going to fly to the arms of my charming Miss Cunegund. My dear Martin, I must insist on it, that Pangloss was in the right. All is for the best."

"I wish it may be," said Martin.

"But this was an odd adventure we met with at Venice. I do not think there ever was an instance before of six dethroned monarchs supping together at a public inn."

"This is not more extraordinary," said Martin, "than most of what has happened to us. It is a very common thing for kings to be dethroned; and as for our having the honor to sup with six of them, it is a mere accident, not deserving our attention."

As soon as Candide set his foot on board the vessel, he flew to his old friend and valet Cacambo and, throwing his arms about his neck, embraced him with transports of joy.

"Well," said he, "what news of Miss Cunegund? Does she still continue the paragon of beauty? Does she love me still? How does she do? You have, doubtless, purchased a superb palace for her at Constantinople."

"My dear master," replied Cacambo, "Miss Cunegund washes dishes on the banks of the Propontis, in the house of a prince who has very few to wash. She is at present a slave in the family of an ancient sovereign named Ragotsky, whom the Grand Turk allows three crowns a day to maintain him in his exile; but the most melancholy circumstance of all is, that she is turned horribly ugly."

"Ugly or handsome," said Candide, "I am a man of honor and, as such, am obliged to love her still. But how could she possibly have been reduced to so abject a condition, when I sent five or six millions to her by you?"

"Lord bless me," said Cacambo, "was not I obliged to give two millions to Seignor Don Fernando d'Ibaraa y Figueora y Mascarenes y Lampourdos y Souza, the Governor of Buenos Ayres, for liberty to take Miss Cunegund away with me? And then did not a brave fellow of a pirate gallantly strip us of all the rest? And then did not this same pirate carry us with him to Cape Matapan, to Milo, to Nicaria, to Samos, to Petra, to the Dardanelles, to Marmora, to Scutari? Miss Cunegund and the old woman are now servants to the prince I have told you of; and I myself am slave to the dethroned Sultan."

"What a chain of shocking accidents!" exclaimed Candide. "But after all, I have still some diamonds left, with which I can easily procure Miss Cunegund's liberty. It is a pity though she is grown so ugly."

Then turning to Martin, "What think you, friend," said he, "whose condition is most to be pitied, the Emperor Achmet's, the Emperor Ivan's, King Charles Edward's, or mine?"

"Faith, I cannot resolve your question," said Martin, "unless I had been in the breasts of you all."

"Ah!" cried Candide, "was Pangloss here now, he would have known, and satisfied me at once."

"I know not," said Martin, "in what balance your Pangloss could have weighed the misfortunes of mankind, and have set a just estimation on their sufferings. All that I pretend to know of the matter is that there are millions of men on the earth, whose conditions are a hundred times more pitiable than those of King Charles Edward, the Emperor Ivan, or Sultan Achmet."

"Why, that may be," answered Candide.

In a few days they reached the Bosphorus; and the first thing Candide did was to pay a high ransom for Cacambo; then, without losing time, he and his companions went on board a galley, in order to search for his Cunegund on the banks of the Propontis, notwithstanding she was grown so ugly.

There were two slaves among the crew of the galley, who rowed very ill, and to whose bare backs the master of the vessel frequently applied a lash. Candide, from natural sympathy, looked at these two slaves more attentively than at any of the rest, and drew near them with an eye of pity. Their features, though greatly disfigured, appeared to him to bear a strong resemblance with those of Pangloss and the unhappy Baron Jesuit, Miss Cunegund's brother. This idea affected him with grief and compassion: he examined them more attentively than before.

"In troth," said he, turning to Martin, "if I had not seen my master Pangloss fairly hanged, and had not myself been unlucky enough to run the Baron through the body, I should absolutely think those two rowers were the men."

No sooner had Candide uttered the names of the Baron and Pangloss, than the two slaves gave a great cry, ceased rowing, and let fall their oars out of their hands. The master of the vessel, seeing this, ran up to them, and redoubled the discipline of the lash.

"Hold, hold," cried Candide, "I will give you what money you shall ask for these two persons."

"Good heavens! it is Candide," said one of the men.

"Candide!" cried the other.

"Do I dream," said Candide, "or am I awake? Am I actually on board this galley? Is this My Lord the Baron, whom I killed? and that my master Pangloss, whom I saw hanged before my face?"

"It is I! it is I!" cried they both together.

"What! is this your great philosopher?" said Martin.

"My dear sir," said Candide to the master of the galley, "how much do you ask for the ransom of the Baron of Thunder–ten–tronckh, who is one of the first barons of the empire, and of Monsieur Pangloss, the most profound metaphysician in Germany?"

"Why, then, Christian cur," replied the Turkish captain, "since these two dogs of Christian slaves are barons and metaphysicians, who no doubt are of high rank in their own country, thou shalt give me fifty thousand sequins."

"You shall have them, sir; carry me back as quick as thought to Constantinople, and you shall receive the money immediately – No!carry me first to Miss Cunegund."

The captain, upon Candide's first proposal, had already tacked about, and he made the crew ply their oars so effectually, that the vessel flew through the water, quicker than a bird cleaves the air.

Candide bestowed a thousand embraces on the Baron and Pangloss. "And so then, my dear Baron, I did not kill you? and you, my dear Pangloss, are come to life again after your hanging? But how came you slaves on board a Turkish galley?"

"And is it true that my dear sister is in this country?" said the Baron.

"Yes," said Cacambo.

"And do I once again behold my dear Candide?" said Pangloss.

Candide presented Martin and Cacambo to them; they embraced each other, and all spoke together. The galley flew like lightning, and soon they were got back to port. Candide instantly sent for a Jew, to whom he sold for fifty thousand sequins a diamond richly worth one hundred thousand, though the fellow swore to him all the time by Father Abraham that he gave him the most he could possibly afford.He no sooner got the money into his hands, than he paid it down for the ransom of the Baron and Pangloss. The latter flung himself at the feet of his deliverer, and bathed him with his tears; the former thanked him with a gracious nod, and promised to return him the money the first opportunity.

"But is it possible," said he, "that my sister should be in Turkey?"

"Nothing is more possible," answered Cacambo, "for she scours the dishes in the house of a Transylvanian prince."

Candide sent directly for two Jews, and sold more diamonds to them; and then he set out with his companions in another galley, to deliver Miss Cunegund from slavery.

CHAPTER 28

What Befell Candide, Cunegund, Pangloss, Martin, etc.

Pardon," said Candide to the Baron; "once more let me entreat your pardon, Reverend Father, for running you through the body."

"Say no more about it," replied the Baron. "I was a little too hasty I must own; but as you seem to be desirous to know by what accident I came to be a slave on board the galley where you saw me, I will inform you. After I had been cured of the wound you gave me, by the College apothecary, I was attacked and carried off by a party of Spanish troops, who clapped me in prison in Buenos Ayres, at the very time my sister was setting out from there. I asked leave to return to Rome, to the general of my Order, who appointed me chaplain to the French Ambassador at Constantinople. I had not been a week in my new office, when I happened to meet one evening a young Icoglan, extremely handsome and well–made. The weather was very hot; the young man had an inclination to bathe. I took the opportunity to bathe likewise. I did not know it was a crime for a Christian to be found naked in company with a young Turk. A cadi ordered me to receive a hundred blows on the soles of my feet, and sent me to the galleys. I do not believe that there was ever an act of more flagrant injustice. But I would fain know how my sister came to be a scullion to a Transylvanian prince, who has taken refuge among the Turks?"

"But how happens it that I behold you again, my dear Pangloss?" said Candide.

"It is true," answered Pangloss, "you saw me hanged, though I ought properly to have been burned; but you may remember, that it rained extremely hard when they were going to roast me. The storm was so violent that they found it impossible to light the fire; so they hanged me because they could do no better. A surgeon purchased my body, carried it home, and prepared to dissect me. He began by making a crucial incision from my navel to the clavicle. It is impossible for anyone to have been more lamely hanged than I had been.The executioner was a subdeacon, and knew how to burn people very well, but as for hanging, he was a novice at it, being quite out of practice; the cord being wet, and not slipping properly, the noose did not join. In short, I still continued to breathe; the crucial incision made me scream to such a degree, that my surgeon fell flat upon his back; and imagining it was the Devil he was dissecting, ran away, and in his fright tumbled down stairs. His wife hearing the noise, flew from the next room, and seeing me stretched upon the table with my crucial incision, was still more terrified than her husband, and fell upon him. When they had a little recovered themselves, I heard her say to her husband, 'My dear, how could you think of dissecting a heretic? Don't you know that the Devil is always in them? I'll run directly to a priest to come and drive the evil spirit out.' I trembled from head to foot at hearing her talk in this manner, and exerted what little strength I had left to cry out, 'Have mercy on me!' At length the Portuguese barber took courage, sewed up my wound, and his wife nursed me; and I was upon my legs in a fortnight's time. The barber got me a place to be lackey to a Knight of Malta, who was going to Venice; but finding my master had no money to pay me my wages, I entered into the service of a Venetian merchant and went with him to Constantinople.

"One day I happened to enter a mosque, where I saw no one but an old man and a very pretty young female devotee, who was telling her beads; her neck was quite bare, and in her bosom she had a beautiful nosegay of tulips, roses, anemones, ranunculuses, hyacinths, and auriculas; she let fall her nosegay. I ran immediately to take it up, and presented it to her with a most respectful bow. I was so long in delivering it that the man began to be angry; and, perceiving I was a Christian, he cried out for help; they carried me before the cadi, who ordered me to receive one hundred bastinadoes, and sent me to the galleys. I was chained in the very galley and to the very same bench with the Baron. On board this galley there were four young men belonging to Marseilles, five Neapolitan priests, and two monks of Corfu, who told us that the like adventures happened every day. The Baron pretended that he had been worse used than myself; and I insisted that there was far less harm in taking up a nosegay, and putting it into a woman's bosom, than to be found stark naked with a young Icoglan. We were continually whipped, and received twenty lashes a day with a heavy thong, when the concatenation of sublunary events brought you on board our galley to ransom us from slavery."

"Well, my dear Pangloss," said Candide to him, "when You were hanged, dissected, whipped, and tugging at the oar, did you continue to think that everything in this world happens for the best?"

"I have always abided by my first opinion," answered Pangloss; "for, after all, I am a philosopher, and it would not become me to retract my sentiments; especially as Leibnitz could not be in the wrong: and that preestablished harmony is the finest thing in the world, as well as a plenum and the materia subtilis."

CHAPTER 29

In What Manner Candide Found Miss Cunegund and the Old Woman Again

While Candide, the Baron, Pangloss, Martin, and Cacambo, were relating their several adventures, and reasoning on the contingent or noncontingent events of this world; on causes and effects; on moral and physical evil; on free will and necessity; and on the consolation that may be felt by a person when a slave and chained to an oar in a Turkish galley, they arrived at the house of the Transylvanian prince on the shores of the Propontis. The first objects they beheld there, were Miss Cunegund and the old woman, who were hanging some tablecloths on a line to dry.

The Baron turned pale at the sight. Even the tender Candide, that affectionate lover, upon seeing his fair Cunegund all sunburned, with bleary eyes, a withered neck, wrinkled face and arms, all covered with a red scurf, started back with horror; but, not withstanding, recovering himself, he advanced towards her out of good manners. She embraced Candide and her brother; they embraced the old woman, and Candide ransomed them both.

There was a small farm in the neighborhood which the old woman proposed to Candide to make shift with till the company should meet with a more favorable destiny. Cunegund, not knowing that she was grown ugly, as no one had informed her of it, reminded Candide of his promise in so peremptory a manner, that the simple lad did not dare to refuse her; he then acquainted the Baron that he was going to marry his sister.

"I will never suffer," said the Baron, "my sister to be guilty of an action so derogatory to her birth and family; nor will I bear this insolence on your part. No, I never will be reproached that my nephews are not qualified for the first ecclesiastical dignities in Germany; nor shall a sister of mine ever be the wife of any person below the rank of Baron of the Empire."

Cunegund flung herself at her brother's feet, and bedewed them with her tears; but he still continued inflexible.

"Thou foolish fellow, said Candide, "have I not delivered thee from the galleys, paid thy ransom, and thy sister's, too, who was a scullion, and is very ugly, and yet condescend to marry her? and shalt thou pretend to oppose the match! If I were to listen only to the dictates of my anger, I should kill thee again."

"Thou mayest kill me again," said the Baron; "but thou shalt not marry my sister while I am living."

CHAPTER 30

Conclusion

Candide had, in truth, no great inclination to marry Miss Cunegund; but the extreme impertinence of the Baron determined him to conclude the match; and Cunegund pressed him so warmly, that he could not recant. He consulted Pangloss, Martin, and the faithful Cacambo. Pangloss composed a fine memorial, by which he proved that the Baron had no right over his sister; and that she might, according to all the laws of the Empire, marry Candide with the left hand. Martin concluded to throw the Baron into the sea; Cacambo decided that he must be delivered to the Turkish captain and sent to the galleys; after which he should be conveyed by the first ship to the Father General at Rome. This advice was found to be good; the old woman approved of it, and not a syllable was said to his sister; the business was executed for a little money; and they had the pleasure of tricking a Jesuit, and punishing the pride of a German baron.

It was altogether natural to imagine, that after undergoing so many disasters, Candide, married to his mistress and living with the philosopher Pangloss, the philosopher Martin, the prudent Cacambo, and the old woman, having besides brought home so many diamonds from the country of the ancient Incas, would lead the most agreeable life in the world. But he had been so robbed by the Jews, that he had nothing left but his little farm; his wife, every day growing more and more ugly, became headstrong and insupportable; the old woman was infirm, and more ill–natured yet than Cunegund. Cacambo, who worked in the garden, and carried the produce of it to sell in Constantinople, was above his labor, and cursed his fate. Pangloss despaired of making a figure in any of the German universities. And as to Martin, he was firmly persuaded that a person is equally ill–situated everywhere.He took things with patience.

Candide, Martin, and Pangloss disputed sometimes about metaphysics and morality. Boats were often seen passing under the windows of the farm laden with effendis, bashaws, and cadis, that were going into banishment to Lemnos, Mytilene and Erzerum. And other cadis, bashaws, and effendis were seen coming back to succeed the place of the exiles, and were driven out in their turns. They saw several heads curiously stuck upon poles, and carried as presents to the Sublime Porte. Such sights gave occasion to frequent dissertations; and when no disputes were in progress, the irksomeness was so excessive that the old woman ventured one day to tell them:

"I would be glad to know which is worst, to be ravished a hundred times by Negro pirates, to have one buttock cut off, to run the gauntlet among the Bulgarians, to be whipped and hanged at an auto–da–fe, to be dissected, to be chained to an oar in a galley; and, in short, to experience all the miseries through which every one of us hath passed, or to remain here doing nothing?"

"This," said Candide, "is a grand question."

This discourse gave birth to new reflections, and Martin especially concluded that man was born to live in the convulsions of disquiet, or in the lethargy of idleness. Though Candide did not absolutely agree to this, yet he did not determine anything on that head. Pangloss avowed that he had undergone dreadful sufferings; but having once maintained that everything went on as well as possible, he still maintained it, and at the same time believed nothing of it.

There was one thing which more than ever confirmed Martin in his detestable principles, made Candide hesitate, and embarrassed Pangloss, which was the arrival of Pacquette and Brother Giroflee one day at their farm. This couple had been in the utmost distress; they had very speedily made away with their three thousand piastres; they had parted, been reconciled; quarreled again, been thrown into prison; had made their escape, and at last Brother Giroflee had turned Turk. Pacquette still continued to follow her trade; but she got little or nothing by it.

"I foresaw very well," said Martin to Candide "that your presents would soon be squandered, and only make them more miserable. You and Cacambo have spent millions of piastres, and yet you are not more happy than Brother Giroflee and Pacquette."

"Ah!" said Pangloss to Pacquette, "it is Heaven that has brought you here among us, my poor child! Do you know that you have cost me the tip of my nose, one eye, and one ear? What a handsome shape is here!and what is this world!"

This new adventure engaged them more deeply than ever in philosophical disputations.

In the neighborhood lived a famous dervish who passed for the best philosopher in Turkey; they went to consult him: Pangloss, who was their spokesman, addressed him thus:

"Master, we come to entreat you to tell us why so strange an animal as man has been formed?"

"Why do you trouble your head about it?" said the dervish; "is it any business of yours?"

"But, Reverend Father," said Candide, "there is a horrible deal of evil on the earth."

"What signifies it," said the dervish, "whether there is evil or good? When His Highness sends a ship to Egypt does he trouble his head whether the rats in the vessel are at their ease or not?"

"What must then be done?" said Pangloss.

"Be silent," answered the dervish.

"I flattered myself," replied Pangloss, "to have reasoned a little with you on the causes and effects, on the best of possible worlds, the origin of evil, the nature of the soul, and a pre–established harmony."

At these words the dervish shut the door in their faces.

During this conversation, news was spread abroad that two viziers of the bench and the mufti had just been strangled at Constantinople, and several of their friends impaled. This catastrophe made a great noise for some hours. Pangloss, Candide, and Martin, as they were returning to the little farm, met with a good–looking old man, who was taking the air at his door, under an alcove formed of the boughs of orange trees. Pangloss, who was as inquisitive as he was disputative, asked him what was the name of the mufti who was lately strangled.

"I cannot tell," answered the good old man; "I never knew the name of any mufti, or vizier breathing. I am entirely ignorant of the event you speak of; I presume that in general such as are concerned in public affairs sometimes come to a miserable end; and that they deserve it: but I never inquire what is doing at Constantinople; I am contented with sending thither the produce of my garden, which I cultivate with my own hands."

After saying these words, he invited the strangers to come into his house. His two daughters and two sons presented them with divers sorts of sherbet of their own making; besides caymac, heightened with the peels of candied citrons, oranges, lemons, pineapples, pistachio nuts, and Mocha coffee unadulterated with the bad coffee of Batavia or the American islands. After which the two daughters of this good Mussulman perfumed the beards of Candide, Pangloss, and Martin.

"You must certainly have a vast estate," said Candide to the Turk.

"I have no more than twenty acres of ground," he replied, "the whole of which I cultivate myself with the help of my children; and our labor keeps off from us three great evils – idleness, vice, and want."

Candide, as he was returning home, made profound reflections on the Turk's discourse.

"This good old man," said he to Pangloss and Martin, "appears to me to have chosen for himself a lot much preferable to that of the six Kings with whom we had the honor to sup."

"Human grandeur," said Pangloss, "is very dangerous, if we believe the testimonies of almost all philosophers; for we find Eglon, King of Moab, was assassinated by Aod; Absalom was hanged by the hair of his head, and run through with three darts; King Nadab, son of Jeroboam, was slain by Baaza; King Ela by Zimri; Okosias by Jehu; Athaliah by Jehoiada; the Kings Jehooiakim, Jeconiah, and Zedekiah, were led into captivity: I need not tell you what was the fate of Croesus, Astyages, Darius, Dionysius of Syracuse, Pyrrhus, Perseus, Hannibal, Jugurtha, Ariovistus, Caesar, Pompey, Nero, Otho, Vitellius, Domitian, Richard II of England, Edward II, Henry VI, Richard Ill, Mary Stuart, Charles I, the three Henrys of France, and the Emperor Henry IV."

"Neither need you tell me," said Candide, "that we must take care of our garden."

"You are in the right," said Pangloss; "for when man was put into the garden of Eden, it was with an intent to dress it; and this proves that man was not born to be idle."

"Work then without disputing," said Martin; "it is the only way to render life supportable."

The little society, one and all, entered into this laudable design and set themselves to exert their different talents. The little piece of ground yielded them a plentiful crop. Cunegund indeed was very ugly, but she became an excellent hand at pastrywork: Pacquette embroidered; the old woman had the care of the linen. There was none, down to Brother Giroflee, but did some service; he was a very good carpenter, and became an honest man. Pangloss used now and then to say to Candide:

"There is a concatenation of all events in the best of possible worlds; for, in short, had you not been kicked out of a fine castle for the love of Miss Cunegund; had you not been put into the Inquisition; had you not traveled over America on foot; had you not run the Baron through the body; and had you not lost all your sheep, which you brought from the good country of El Dorado, you would not have been here to eat preserved citrons and pistachio nuts."

"Excellently observed," answered Candide; "but let us cultivate our garden."

— THE END —